Once upon a time...

Hmm, kids keep asking me to write a mystery book. What shall I do?

Mimi

Write one about spiders!

You two really are characters, that's all I've got to say!

Yes you are! And, of course I choose you! But what should I write about?

National Parks!

Scary Places!

Famous Places!

Fun Places!

Disney World!

New York City!

Dracula's Castle

GRAND CANYON

7

On the *Mystery Girl* airplane ...

I CAN FLY US ANYWHERE!

Or aboard the *Mimi!*

Take me to the Forbidden City!

Or by surfboard, rickshaw, motorbike, camel ...

All great ideas! I can put a lot of history, **MYSTERY,** legend, lore, and **laughs** in the books! We can use other boys and girls in the books. It will be educational and fun!

Good stuff!

Where will you get the other kids, Mimi?

From my Fan Club! Kids can apply to be characters!

And can you put some cool stuff online? Like a Book Club and a Scavenger Hunt and a Map so we can track our adventures?

Of course!

And can cousins Avery and Ella and Evan and some of our friends be in the books?

Of course!

9

Can I apply?

The *Mystery Girl* is all revved up—let's go!

You mean now?

LET'S GO!

And so, Mimi, Papa, Christina, and Grant took off aboard the *Mystery Girl* and America's National Mystery Book Series—where the adventure is real and so are the characters! —was born.

START YOUR ADVENTURE TODAY!

READ THE BOOK!

GO ONLINE!

TRACK YOUR ADVENTURES!

APPLY TO BE A CHARACTER!

Yikes! That was close!

Rats!

ABOUT THE CHARACTERS

Christina
Yother
Age 9

Grant
Yother
Age 7

Alexis
DeJoy
Age 12

Griffin
DeJoy
Age 10

Child of Flight

Mr. Orville, Mr. Wilbur, all of us up early;
Me and the grown up men
Left the lifesaving station—
Would there be a life to save on the sand?

What is this flying all about, I wonder;
Birds and kites, I can see, but men?
Mr. Orville, Mr. Wilbur, they believe

Ice on the ground, frost in the air;
Mr. Orville, Mr. Wilbur, they shake hands;
The machine they call Flyer sits on the sand;
Now a man climbs aboard;
Machine and man seem one

The noise of the engine, the noise of the wind;
We tug the Flyer along its track until, until,
Until . . .It lets loose upon the sky!

Mr. Orville, Mr. Wilbur, what have they done?
Dad says made history, all will change.
Me and the grown up men
Trudge through the sand

Back to the lifesaving station,
I note in the log:
Mr. Orville, Mr. Wilbur fly at Kitty Hawk;
No lives lost today

– Carole Marsh

1

MAN WILL NEVER FLY

Grant, Christina, Mimi and Papa stood and looked at the little red airplane. It had *My Girl* written on the side in cursive.

"Are we all packed?" Papa asked.

"Everything's stowed away, captain," said Mimi.

Grant and Christina giggled. Their grandfather had only recently gotten his pilot's license and was flying them to North Carolina for the big 100th anniversary of the First Flight celebration. It was going to be a BIG DEAL. Her grandmother had been writing books about the Wright brothers' incredible first manned flight for more than a year.

"Then all aboard!" Papa said.

"Don't you have your planes and your trains all mixed up?" Christina teased Papa.

Papa roared with laughter. "Planes, trains, automobiles, camels, donkeys, rickshaws—whatever it takes, we're going to be in Kill Devil Hills in time for the whole shebang," he promised.

The "whole shebang" was supposed to be everything you could imagine to celebrate the "First Flight." The president of the United States was coming. So was the aircraft carrier *Kitty Hawk*. There was going to be a big flyover of all kinds of aircraft—including old-fashioned barnstormers, as well as the latest spy planes! And, most special, a **replica** of *Flyer*, Orville and Wilbur Wright's first real airplane, was going to be flown over the sand dunes at Kill Devil Hills.

Of course, thought Christina, Mimi was most excited about the Black and White "First Flight" Ball! Her ball gown was beautiful—all black satin with white trim and sparkly crystal stones. She swore she was going to wear red shoes beneath it, for good luck. Christina sure wished *she* was going to the ball. She looked over at Grant who was strapped in and wide-eyed. He had never flown in a plane this small before, and he looked a little scared.

"It's ok, Grant," Christina told her younger brother, who was seven. Christina was nine and liked to think she had seen it all, although she knew she had not. However, she *had* seen a lot since she and her brother often gallivanted across the United States with their grandparents. Mimi wrote mystery books for kids and often included her grandchildren, their friends, and members of her Carole Marsh Mysteries fan club in the books.

They had been a lot of cool places, always having fun . . . and almost always getting in trouble before it was over with. Of course, Mimi usually put all that in the books, so it was ok. She called it "research." Grant and Christina called it getting out of school with a neat excuse!

On this trip to the Outer Banks of North Carolina, they were going to meet up with their Tarheel cousins Alex and Griffin. Alex (short for Alexis) was almost 13 and Griffin was 10. They were a lot of fun to be around. Christina was envious that they got to live at the beach year-round. They always had tans and windblown hair. They knew how to surf and hang glide and all of that beachy keen stuff. Christina hoped they would teach her some of that this year. She was not used to going to the beach in the winter, though. Why couldn't Orville and Wilbur have made their famous first flight in the summer, she thought.

Suddenly, Papa revved the engines and the shiny propellers began to spin. The Halloween orange windsock at Falcon Field seemed to satisfy Papa that it was "all systems go." Christina thought her grandfather would have made a good astronaut. When she told him that, he said, "I might yet, kiddo!"

They waved goodbye to their family—Mom, Dad, Uncle Michael, Aunt Cassidy, and their shiny, pink, new baby girl, Avery Elizabeth. Christina couldn't wait until Avery—or "Duckie," as Mimi called her because she had so many outfits with ducks on them, was old enough to join them on trips like this.

As the little plane began to speed across the tarmac, Grant grabbed his sister by the hand. "Hey," he yelled over the noise of the engine. "Don't Mimi and Papa belong to the Man Will Never Fly Society?"

"Yes," Christina screamed back at him. The adults in front could not even hear them.

"Then," said Grant, "if man will never fly, what are we doing in this contraption?"

Christina laughed. "Oh, Grant, you've flown on airplanes before. Lots of times."

"I kknow," said Grant, his voice stuttering as the plane's wheels seemed to bounce across the runway. "Bbut they were BIG. This thing ffeels llike a rrocking hhorse."

Christina held her brother's hand tighter as the airplane suddenly swooshed smoothly up into the air. A little turbulence rocked them left and right as they pulled up into the sky. As Papa banked into a turn over the beautiful forested city where they lived—Peachtree City, Georgia—Grant seemed to relax. He let his sister's hand drop and stretched and yawned as though the takeoff had been a piece of cake.

"I guess man *will* fly," Grant admitted.

"Well, thousands of people are sure counting on it in North Carolina this week," Christina said, fishing around in her backpack for some pretzels.

As he leveled the airplane, Papa glanced back at his two grandchildren. "Orville and Wilbur, here we come!" he said.

Everyone, including Mimi, laughed. That's because they had no way of knowing that they were flying into the strangest mystery they had ever encountered, and that the fate of the BIG DEAL celebration would be up to four kids.

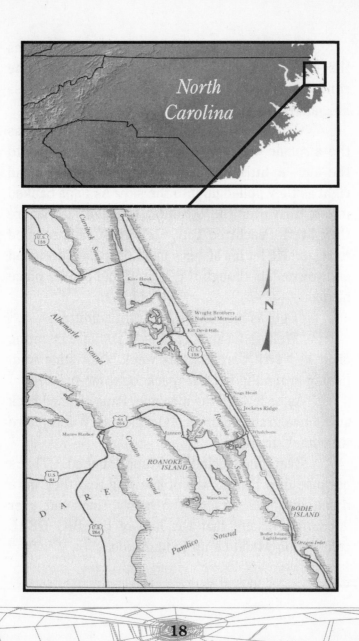

2

MEET ME IN MANTEO

Christina thought it was fun to fly low over the North Carolina coast. Papa called it flying "nap of the earth."

Even though there had been patchy fog over Georgia and South Carolina, by the time they crossed into North Carolina, it was a beautiful sunny December morning. The land below looked like a quilt (a *counterpane*, Mimi called it) of patches of farmland stitched together with shiny silver threads of streams and rivers.

As they flew up the coastline, Christina and Grant craned their necks to see the long ribbon of beige sand pummeled by the white waves of the Atlantic Ocean. Christina knew from reading Mimi's *The Mystery of Blackbeard the Pirate* that this area had once been known as the Graveyard of the Atlantic because of all the shipwrecks that had taken place before lighthouses were installed on all the dangerous points of land jutting out into the water.

"There's Cape Hatteras!" Papa cried, tilting the plane a little so they could see better. The Hatteras Lighthouse was the tallest on this coast, and had black and white spiral stripes. It had been moved—standing straight up!—inland a little ways to protect it from the erosion that threatened to topple over the historic landmark.

"And there's Chicamacomico Lifesaving Station," Mimi added, pointing to a clapboard building up ahead. She told her grandchildren that people who lived along the coast had often served as **involuntary** "life savers" when ships wrecked just offshore.

"Weren't they afraid they would drown going out in the stormy ocean to try to save total strangers?" Christina asked. Mimi said, "Their motto was You Don't Have to Come Back . . . You Just Have to Go Out."

Christina was glad that today there was the U.S. Coast Guard. In fact, off the port (left) side of the plane Papa pointed out *Pedro*, the famous orange Coast Guard rescue "chopper."

Before Christina knew it, they were coming in for a landing at Dare County Airport. As soon as they touched down, Christina felt like their First Flight adventure had begun. There were a lot more airplanes and people around than usual. This time of year, Papa said, this part of the coast was usually a ghost town. But it was obvious from the banners and balloons and bands at practice on the tarmac that something special was going to happen.

"*Terra firma!*" said Mimi, as she stepped off the little steps of the airplane onto the ground.

"What's that?" Grant asked, bouncing down the steps behind her.

"That's Latin for good old mother earth!" Mimi said.

Christina followed Grant, and they headed toward the small terminal. Papa stayed behind to secure the plane and bring the rest of their baggage.

"Welcome to Manteo!" said an official First Flight greeter, as they entered the terminal.

Mimi smiled at the greeter but kept marching on. Christina knew where she was headed—to the coffee shop. They each climbed up on a tall stool at a counter overlooking the runways. Mimi ordered a *café latté,* and Grant and Christina ordered milkshakes.

"Didn't people ever fly before the Wright brothers?" Christina asked her grandmother.

Mimi answered in her storyteller voice. "The history of flight is a long one," she said. Christina and Grant groaned. When they wanted a short answer, Mimi always gave them a long one, but at least this answer should be pretty interesting.

"Think about it!" Mimi continued. "People watched birds fly, and wondered if man could learn to fly too. A very long time ago, a Spanish doctor attached wings to his body and tried to fly—but he crashed."

Christina and Grant laughed. "That sounds too silly to be true," Christina said.

"Oh, there were a lot of silly things leading up to the First Flight," Mimi assured them. "People tried all kinds of ways to fly and they flopped. But you have to start somewhere, you know, when you're trying to invent something new."

"So did *anybody* ever get off the ground?" asked Grant, zooming his had around the air like a plane.

"The first successful flight in a hot air balloon was made in 1783," Mimi said. "There were a lot of designs on paper, but building an airplane that could actually fly . . . well, that was a sticky wicket!"

"A *what*?" Christina asked.

Mimi laughed. "A real problem," she explained.

"But the Wright brothers figured it out, right Mimi?" Grant asked.

"Not so fast, young man!" Mimi said. "They finally did, but it took them years of hard work and sacrifice. Then, they came down to the North Carolina coast because it had the best wind . . ."

". . . And a soft place to land?" Christina interrupted.

"Well, not sooooo soft," said Mimi, "but yes— the sand dunes of Kill Devil Hills at Kitty Hawk were a perfect place for their experiment."

"An experiment?" asked Grant.

But before Mimi could answer, they heard a big giant *SLURRRRRRP* as Papa came up behind them and leaned over and finished their milkshakes. His grandkids frowned at him.

"That's right," said Papa, wiping chocolate foam from his upper lip. "Orville and Wilbur had to try and fail and try again—*many times* before they were successful."

"But then," Mimi finished the story with a grand swish of her coffee cup through the air, "on December 17, 1903, the Wright brothers became the first people to fly a plane that was heavier than air . . . using power . . . and stay aloft, fly ahead, and safely land!"

"Wow!" Christina exclaimed, trying to imagine how exciting, and maybe even scary, that must have been.

"Hey, that's 100 years ago!" Grant said.

Everyone laughed. "Well, duh," Christina teased her brother. "Ye-ah. That's why we're here. To celebrate the 100th anniversary of the First Flight."

Mimi frowned at her granddaughter. "Be polite," she warned. To Grant she said, "You were smart to do that math in your head, Grant. Maybe *you* can grow up and invent something?"

Grant folded his arms and frowned like he always did when someone had hurt his feelings. "Duh. Ye-ah. Maybe I can invent a sister-squashing-machine."

Now Mimi frowned at her grandson. Papa frowned at them all. "Hey, you hooligans!" he said. "We're here to have fun. Let's not argue. Let's go to town and eat lunch. My treat!"

Mimi and the kids laughed. "Papa, you *always* treat!" Christina said.

"Duh. Ye-ah," said Papa, leading them across the terminal lobby. "But one day, after you invent some amazing invention and get rich—then *you* can treat!" he told his grandchildren.

As they laughed and followed Papa out of the airport, none of them noticed that the friendly greeter now sneered at them. She held a key in her hand and laughed meanly as she headed out the door and across the tarmac to *My Girl.*

3

JOCKEY'S RIDGE

Papa had rented them a red Jeep. They piled in with their red (Papa), white (Mimi) and blue (Christina and Grant) sweaters on.

"Hey, we look pretty patriotic!" Papa noted as he started the engine.

"Put this sunblock on!" Mimi insisted, passing a squirt tube around.

"You can't get sunburned in winter, can you?" Grant asked, rubbing wayyyyy too much of the white stuff over his face. He looked like a messy ghost.

"Sure you can," said Christina. "Remember that year we went snow skiing and Papa got his face all sunburned?"

"Thanks for reminding me," Papa said.

"Sorry, Papa," said Christina, "but you did look pretty funny."

"Well, there's nothing funny about sunburn," Mimi said, rubbing the rest of Grant's goo into his skin. He tried to pull away.

The wind buffeted the car as they drove to town. The Outer Banks had always been known for its steady breezes. That's what kept vacationers coming in the hot summer, and that's what brought the Wright brothers here.

At the Oyster Bar on the causeway, they got a seat in a booth by the windows that looked back across Roanoke Sound. It was a crystal clear day, and they could see all the way across the water to the enormous sand dunes sticking up like gigantic scoops of vanilla ice cream.

Christina pointed toward the largest dune. "Is that Kill Devil Hills?" she asked.

"That's Jockey's Ridge," said Papa. "It's the largest sand dune on the Atlantic coast. Horse races were once held at the base. Today, hang gliders love to take-off from the top."

"Heeey," said Grant. "Hang gliding! That's what I want to do."

"You're probably too little for that," Christina said, looking at Papa.

"That's true," said Papa. "That sand is not as soft as it looks—if you went splat on it, it would really hurt!"

"Phooey," said Grant. "How come I'm too little to fly?"

"Oh, I didn't say that!" said Papa. "In the air show later this week, you'll see kids as young as you fly real airplanes."

The waitress brought icy, sweating glasses of lemonade. As they slurped the cool sweet and sour drinks, Christina tried to imagine flying an airplane. Or a hot air balloon. Or even a hang glider. She decided she was not quite that brave.

"Were Orville and Wilbur kids when they learned to fly?" Christina asked.

"In a way," said Mimi. "They were about your age when their Dad bought them a toy helicopter. It was only made of folded paper, but it planted the seed in their minds that perhaps man could fly—and maybe they could prove it."

"Why do you and Papa belong to the Man Can Never Fly Society?" Grant asked.

Mimi and Papa laughed. "It's sort of a joke," Mimi said.

"You know," said Papa. "People sometimes say if God had meant for man to fly, he would have given them wings."

Christina and Grant thought about that for awhile, then Christina snapped her fingers. "Eureka!" she cried. "He did give us wings! Airplane wings!"

Mimi nodded. "That's right! Saying that Man Will Never Fly is sort of a reminder to us all that nothing's impossible—you just have to believe that you can make it happen."

"Like going to Mars!" said Grant.

"Or making an A in math," said Christina.

"That's right," said Mimi. "Whatever your dream is, you have to stick to it."

"And you have to work hard," said Papa. "Real hard."

The waitress reappeared with steaming bowls of clam chowder. She also put down a basket of hot hush puppies, which Christina and Grant loved. Grant squirted a big blob of ketchup on his plate and dunked a hush puppy into it. "How did hush puppies get their name?"

"You remember," said Christina, squirting her name in ketchup cursive in the middle of her plate. "Papa told us that in the Civil War soldiers would throw fried cornbread to the dogs to keep them from barking and giving away their position to the enemy."

"Yeah," Grant recalled. "And they said 'Hush Puppies!'"

Mimi laughed. "You puppies hush up and eat, and I'll tell you about the time the sand dunes ate a hotel!"

"Aw, Mimi, you're making that one up," Christina said.

"Am not!" insisted Mimi. "The dunes are always shifting. Once they finally moved right up and over an old inn until it disappeared beneath the sand."

"Sounds like kudzu," said Papa. He meant the vine that often covered trees and telephone poles beside the roads in the South. Kudzu was originally imported from Japan for soil erosion and can grow as much as 12 inches in a single day.

"Kudzu please pass the ketchup?" asked Grant. Only it sounded more like, "Kudph zoo pleath path thu kethup," because his mouth was so full of hush puppies that his cheeks poked out like a squirrel's that was full of nuts.

"Let's finish eating so we can check in at the inn and get a good room," Mimi said.

Christina spied a woman at the next table giving her the Evil Eye. That's really suspicious, Christina thought to herself. Why would a stranger look at me so meanly? Christina solved the problem by looking out at the beautiful blue water with its twinkling whitecaps as she finished her lunch.

But when they left the restaurant, the stranger followed behind them.

4
THE NOT SO TRANQUIL HOUSE INN

The inn where they were staying was right on the water in the village of Manteo. The room they had requested looked out across the water to the *Elizabeth II*. The "Lizzy II" was a replica of the ship that brought the first English colonists to the New World. Christina knew all about the ship because Mimi had once written a kid's book—*The Mystery of the Lost Colony*—about it.

Christina loved the sprawling inn with its porches and balconies, which were covered in tiny yellow roses. While Papa checked in and carried the baggage to their room, the kids and their grandmother sat in oversized rockers on the front porch beneath whirring paddle fans.

"Mimi, what did you say happened to the Lost Colonists?" Christina asked dreamily.

Mimi laughed. "We don't know!" she said. "That's why we say they're lost!"

Grant looked really puzzled, so Mimi explained. "The English colonists came to this part of the New World more than 400 years ago. They said the oysters were as big as a man's forearm, and the mosquitoes were as large as a dinner plate! They brought women and children with them and set up camp in a palisaded fort they built from scratch."

"The Indians still lived here then?" Grant guessed.

"Oh, yes," said Mimi. "This was their home. They were mostly friendly to the newcomers, but the colonists weren't always so friendly to them. For one thing, the Native Americans had no immunity to the 'white man's' diseases, and so the local Indians were suspicious when they began to die of illnesses they had never seen before."

"What happened?" Christina asked, trying to imagine coming to a strange, new land and set up housekeeping among "the savages," as they had called the native peoples.

"Well," said Mimi. "When a ship came to bring supplies, the colonists had vanished!"

"Didn't they leave a note saying where they were going?" Grant asked.

"Sort of," Mimi said. "On a tree they carved the word CROATAN."

"Which meant?" Christina asked.

"Good question!" said Mimi. "If the rescue party had known that, they might have found the colonists."

"Maybe they went to live on some other island," Grant speculated.

"Or to live with the Indians," guessed Christina, who liked happy endings."

"Or maybe they all were killed," said Grant, sadly.

"Or maybe we just don't know," said Mimi. "And that's why that history is still a mystery till this day!"

History was *always* a mystery to Christina. Why did people always have to fight? Why were there wars? Why was Papa looking so mysterious himself, she wondered, as her grandfather came up the stairs and gave Mimi a sheepish look.

"No room in the inn," he said.

"WHAT?!" cried Mimi. Her face got red.

Papa calmed her down. "They mistakenly gave our room away, but I've made other arrangements." Papa gave Christina and Grant a wink. Papa was good at making "other arrangements," but they wondered what in the world this would be—ALL the hotels had been booked up for months and months for the First Flight celebration.

Mimi gave Papa her special look which meant "this had better be good." Papa gave her a big smacky kiss on the cheek to indicate that she was going to love his "arrangement." "We're staying . . ." he began dramatically, then finished with a great flourish of his arm waving toward the beach, "at Orville and Wilbur's house!"

Grant didn't know what that meant, but he was excited anyway. "Yipee! Hurrah!! Wow!!! Let's go!!!!"

Christina was more skeptical. "Go where?" she asked quietly. She liked the inn; she didn't want to leave.

Mimi pouted. "This better be good," she warned Papa.

Papa had a funny look on his face, like maybe he had made a bad boo boo. "Hmm," he said, taking Mimi's hand and pulling her up out of the rocker. "Maybe I had better show you."

The guys bounded down the steps. The girls trudged along behind them. As they piled into the Jeep, Christina thought she might cry as they drove through the little village. She gave the Lizzy II a secret wave goodbye. She groaned as they passed

Manteo Booksellers, her favorite kind of bookstore—
it had big armchairs where you could sit and read
part of a book to see if you liked it before you
bought it.

Mimi groaned as they passed the giant
Christmas Shop where she loved to buy ornaments.
They rode in silence back across the causeway. Was
their special vacation already ruined even before it
began? Mimi always said you had to "roll with the
punches," but this felt like a sucker punch to
Christina's gut. Oh, well, at least they were headed
for the beach.

But Papa turned before the beach road and
Christina watched the little milepost signs whisk by
as they headed north. What she didn't notice was
the car tailing them. The "official" First Flight
greeter drove; the strange woman from the
restaurant rode in the passenger seat. She had an
angry scowl on her face.

5
KITTY HAWK

When they passed the milepost marker that said Kitty Hawk, Papa slowed down. It was still a couple of days before the big 100th anniversary air show and celebration, so there was not very much traffic on the roads yet. What there was all seemed to be headed to the same place—the Wright Brothers National Memorial.

When Papa put on his turn signal and got into the turning lane, Mimi looked puzzled. "We're going to the memorial now?" she asked.

"Uh, yes," said Papa.

Christina and Grant looked out at the famous site. The sand dunes where the famous First Flight was made spread out before them. On top of a hill was the large monument dedicated to the Wright Brothers' feat. To the right was the memorial museum. In the center were a few makeshift tents and buildings that looked like they had been there a hundred years.

Without speaking, Papa drove slowly along the long, winding road until he came to one of the far tents. He stopped the car.

Mimi looked at him suspiciously. "And why are we stopping *here*?" she asked, in her maybe-I'm-about-to-be-angry voice.

Papa looked at Mimi with his big blue eyes and smiled. "Uh, this is where we're staying."

In the back seat, Christina and Grant could hardly believe their ears. "Wow!" said Christina. "We're going to stay right here in the park—that's exciting!"

"Double wow!" squealed Grant. "We're going to camp out!"

"*Camp out?!*" Mimi repeated, in a tone that indicated that she could not believe her ears either.

The kids hopped out of the car and dashed across the sand toward the large tent. Christina looked back to see if her grandparents were coming. However, they just sat in the car. From a distance, it sounded like they were arguing.

As the kids approached the tent, they were surprised to see a man, a boy, and a girl suddenly pop out from the tent's flap door.

"Welcome!" said the man. It was Uncle Joe and their cousins Griffin and Alex. Everyone hugged everyone.

Alex smiled at Grant and Christina. "I hear you're going to stay with us."

Christina's mouth fell open. Her big, blue eyes got even bigger. "Stay with you?"

"Sure," said Alex. "Here in the tent. Dad's got it fixed up nice."

"Barracks style, of course!" added Griffin. He held the tent flap open. When they went inside, the light was dim and it took a few moments for their eyes to adjust. The tent was a large, roomy rectangle. It had a peaked roof held up by several poles. It even had windows with screens in them, their flaps pulled back to let in the light and air.

Alex showed them around. "This is the galley," she said, indicating a round camp table surrounded by deck chairs. There were cupboards, a small refrigerator, and a microwave.

"And this is Dad's work bench," Griffin said proudly.

"What's he making?" asked Grant, lifting his hand to touch one of the many tools sitting on the wooden table.

"Uh, don't do that!" Griffin warned. "We aren't allowed to touch Dad's tools. They're real antiques."

"He's making antiques?" Grant asked, confused.

"No," explained Alex. "He's one of the historic preservationists on the site for the 100th anniversary celebration of the Wright brothers' first flight. He's helping on the replica of *Flyer*—Orville and Wilbur's plane," she added proudly.

"They're going to fly it at the celebration!" said Griffin. "Just like they did 100 years ago."

Christina looked through the screened window where she could see the small airplane of wood and fabric that was nearly the color of the sand. "That thing's gonna fly?"

"You bet!" said Uncle Joe, ushering Mimi and Papa into the tent.

"Well, well," said Papa, admiringly. He looked through the window at the plane. "She's a real beauty! That re-enactment of the first flight will be the hit of the entire celebration."

"Well, well," said Mimi, not admiringly at all. "So this is where I'm going to sleep?" She indicated the row of cots at the back of the tent.

The men laughed. "Afraid so," said Papa. "I told you all the rooms were taken. Joe offered his hospitality, and well, I thought the kids would love being this close to the action." He looked at Mimi. "And I thought you might get into the spirit of things," he added, hopefully.

Mimi gave Christina a wink. "Sand in my red dancing shoes. Sounds marvelous!"

Everyone laughed, except Uncle Joe.

"Hey, Joe, what's the matter?" Papa asked. "Afraid to fly?"

Uncle Joe sat down on the stool in front of his work bench and sighed. "No, of course not," he said. "I'm just worried. Everything has been so perfect, but this week . . ." He stopped talking and looked dreamily out the window at *Flyer*.

"This week, what?" asked Mimi.

Uncle Joe frowned. "This week, we've had some vandalism. Someone broke into the tent and stole some of my tools. There have been some tie-downs around the airplanes missing. Just little stuff. But it worries me. I can't imagine who is behind these pranks. Or why."

As Mimi headed toward an empty cot, she said, "Oh, don't worry. Maybe you just have First Flight jitters. It's probably just some bored kids."

"Hey!" grumbled Christina. "Don't blame kids, Mimi."

Mimi laughed. "Sorry," she said. "You're right—that wasn't fair. It could be anyone. But if they get caught, they will be in B.T."

Alex and Griffin looked confused, but Christina whispered the explanation. "Big Trouble!" They nodded in understanding.

Uncle Joe shook his head. "I'm not worried that they'll get caught," he admitted solemnly. "I'm worried that they won't."

"And do something worse?" Grant guessed.

Uncle Joe nodded. "And as your Papa will tell you, you can't mess around with airplanes."

"Not if you want them to go uppity up up instead of down diddity down down," said Christina.

Uncle Joe stood up, looking angry. "Not if you want this celebration to come off without a hitch," he said. "People have been working for years to get ready for this event. People are coming from all over the world. Everyone wants everything to be perfect," he said.

Mimi shook her head slowly. "Well," she said, "apparently, not *everyone*."

"Hey!" said Papa, changing the subject. "Stow your stuff in your bunk and put on your swimsuits and let's go to the beach!"

When they were ready and left the tent, Uncle Joe put a padlock on the flap door. As they headed for his sand-colored Jeep, Christina did not notice that the suspicious car that had followed them down the highway had also followed them into the park. The two women had stopped near the monument on top of the hill. From behind the large, stone structure strutted another woman. She wore dirty jeans and a work shirt. Her hair was windblown and freckles dotted her nose and cheeks. She looked very smug as she nodded to the other two women and jumped into the back seat of their rusted Jeep. The car took off into the dunes with a squeal of tires, spewing a rooster's tail of sand.

6
THE BEACH

Christina adored the beach. So did her brother. Alex and Griffin were absolute beach bums, she noted. While she and Grant were pale faces, Alex and Griffin had dark tans. Christina and Grant had new bathing suits. Alex and Griffin had suits that looked like all the colors had washed out of them and out to sea.

"We swim everyday!" said Alex, diving into an oncoming wave head first.

"C'mon, Grant," Griffin cried. "I'll teach you to surf." He lugged a surfboard twice as long as he was tall out into the waves.

Christina and Grant sat on the beach and watched their cousins jealously. But it was hard to be upset at the beach, Christina thought. She stretched out on her beach towel and felt the warm sun on her skin. Grant stood in the shallows and cheered Griffin to, "Hang ten!"

The adults sat nearby. "It's surprisingly warm for December," said Mimi.

"That's because a storm front may be coming through," said Uncle Joe. He sounded nervous.

"You don't mean a Nor'easter?" said Papa. Northeasters were storms that often came screaming down the coast in the winter. They caused a lot of damage. Sometimes, the beach was eroded so badly that some of the front row beach houses were washed away.

Uncle Joe just looked at Papa. Mimi got suspicious. "You don't mean a *hurricane*? Hurricanes don't come in the winter, do they?"

"Not usually," said Uncle Joe. "Hurricane season is from June to November. But the hurricanes don't know that. There have been winter hurricanes before. The tropical disturbance we're watching offshore is certainly suspicious. But it would have to get a lot stronger to be any kind of threat."

Christina, as usual, was eavesdropping. She picked up her head off her folded arms. "Threat? What kind of threat?"

"Well, you can't exactly have an air show in the middle of a hurricane," said Papa.

The beach in winter

"And you'd have to evacuate all the people," said Mimi.

Christina looked at Mimi. Mimi looked at Christina. Together, they both cried, "Yiiiiiiiiiiiiiiii!"

"What's wrong?" Papa demanded.

Christina knew what Mimi was going to say. "They'd have to cancel the Ball!"

Papa and Joe groaned, but Mimi and Christina laughed. Christina laughed so hard that she rolled over and over in the sand until she hit the cold water. It felt really icy. She jumped up and grabbed her brother's hand and tugged him out into the water. "C'mon, Grant," she said. "Let's go ride the waves. We can do that." And soon all four kids were splashing and having a ball of their own in the chilly winter ocean.

When they finally crawled out of the water, they were very tired. Each body was pimpled with goosebumps. The towels that had been sitting in the sun felt nice and warm when they wrapped up in them. As dusk settled in, it got even cooler. Papa and Uncle Joe built a big bonfire of driftwood. Mimi had brought marshmallows, which they stuck on driftwood sticks and roasted over the blazing fire. She also had brought a thermos of cocoa.

As they huddled around the fire in their towels, eating and drinking, Christina asked Uncle Joe and Papa to tell them stories of the old Outer Banks. Especially how it got its unusual names. They made it like a game.

"Nag's Head!" said Griffin. "Dad."

Uncle Joe shook his head and rubbed his chin as if he were thinking, but the kids knew he was just teasing and had the answer all along.

Finally, he said, "Most people believe Nags Head got its name like this: Shipwrecked pirates became stranded along the shore with no way to make a living. So, they would tie a lantern around the neck of one of the wild ponies that lived here. Then they would lead the pony up onto the sand dunes. Lookouts in their crow's nest on ships offshore would spy the light. Believing it to be a port, they would steer for it—only to founder on the shoals. After the ship wrecked, the pirates plundered the goods that washed ashore."

"That was pretty sneaky," said Grant.

"It was really mean," Christina agreed.

"Yes," said Uncle Joe, "but back then, this coast was a desolate place. You had to survive any way you could."

Mimi said, "There are still some pretty odd characters living on the Outer Banks!"

Papa agreed. "Yes, like foolish people who sit on the beach in winter and freeze to death!"

The kids nodded as they shivered. It was turning increasingly colder. Uncle Joe looked at the glowering sky and shook his head. "I'd better get back and check *Flyer*," he said. It was clear to them all that the plane was his baby, and he was its guardian angel until it took its own "first flight."

Quickly, they gathered their things. The men threw sand on the smoldering fire. They crowded into the Jeep and pulled onto the highway at Milepost 9. Christina loved that you could drive on the beach in winter. She also loved the magical sight of the fingernail of moon over the Wright Brothers' monument as they drove into the park.

The kids yawned. Their tummies rumbled. It would be good to get clean and dry and warm and go eat shrimpburgers at Sam and Omie's.

But when Uncle Joe made the turn toward the tent, he slammed on the brakes and the Jeep fishtailed in the sand. The skid brought them to a sudden halt and they all bumped into one another.

"What's wrong?" demanded Mimi. She did not like reckless driving.

Uncle Joe just stared straight ahead. The vehicle's headlights made two large puddles of light out on the sand. They could hardly hear the man when he spoke. "The plane is gone," he whispered.. *"Flyer's* GONE!"

7
FLYER FLEW THE COOP

It *was* hard to believe. How could something as big as an airplane, even a little airplane, disappear? Christina didn't know the answer and she could tell from the dumbfounded look on everyone else's faces, they had no clue either.

"Maybe it's a trick," said Grant. "Like those magicians on TV who make big things disappear—right before your eyes!"

"This isn't a trick," said Griffin. *"Flyer* is really gone."

Uncle Joe finally cut the engine, and they sat in silence staring at the empty lake of light. "This is strange," he finally said. "Where is security?"

Simultaneously, Uncle Joe and Papa hopped out of the Jeep and dashed around. They called to the other tents, but no one answered.

Uncle Joe banged on the security shed door, but no one answered. Papa cried into the night, "Is anyone here?!"

There was no answer. "Only us chickens," Mimi said quietly.

"What, Mimi?" Christina asked.

Mimi shook her head. "Oh, it's just an old expression." She opened the car door and jumped out. "C'mon. We can't do anything about this mystery right now. So let's get you kids inside before you catch your death of cold."

Eagerly, the children tumbled out onto the sand. Uncle Joe and Papa had vanished into the darkness. Mimi headed for the tent. As she reached in the darkness for the flap, she groaned.

"Something wrong?" asked Alex.

"Oh, I forgot about the padlock and your dad has the key," said Mimi.

"Ouch!" Grant suddenly cried.

"What's wrong with you?" Griffin said. "You can't stump your toe in the sand."

"Well I sure did," Grant grumbled. He reached down to pick up the rock or whatever object that he had stepped on. It was the padlock. The chain was broken in two.

Mimi yanked the flap open, and the kids dashed inside. In the dim light, they peered around to see if everything was all right. Mimi could spot nothing out of the ordinary, except an overturned chair. She herded the kids toward their cots.

"Rinse off quickly and put on your pajamas."

Christina moaned and held her stomach. "We're not going out to eat?"

"No," said Mimi. "We're *camping out*, remember," she said grimly. "I'm making scrambled egg sandwiches."

She lit the lantern in the galley and began to fiddle with the camp stove. The kids scampered away to obey her. And soon, they were all gathered around the little table eating hot bacon and egg sandwiches (really sort of "sand" wiches since you could feel a little bit of grit in each bite) and drinking cold glasses of milk.

Christina could feel that they were all nervous. It was dark and quiet out here on the lonesome sand dunes. The wind had picked up and was whining around the corner of the tent like a disgruntled ghost. "Can we continue the game?" she asked.

Mimi nodded. "Name a place, Alex," she said.

Alex looked thoughtful. "Blackbeard," she said.

"Hey, that's not a place!" Griffin complained.

"I don't care," said Alex. "I want to hear about Blackbeard!"

"Ok, ok!" Mimi said, trying to keep the peace. "I'll tell, I'll tell! After all, you're holding me hostage on this sand dune," she groused.

The kids laughed. Everyone relaxed a little, and Mimi began her tale of the fiercest pirate of them all:

"'Only me and the devil know where my treasure is,' Blackbeard once bragged," Mimi said. "'And may the one who has the longest liver take it all!'"

The kids laughed so hard that egg spewed right out of their mouths. "Mimi!" said Christina. "You mean the one who lives the longest, don't you?"

"Oh, I guess I do," Mimi said with a smile. "But don't you just wonder what Blackbeard did with all that booty he plundered all those years? Could it be hidden beneath one of these sand dunes?"

Quietly, the children thought about that. Finally, Grant asked, "Did Blackbeard really eat gunpowder for breakfast?"

"It is said he did," said Mimi. "And he had 14 wives. And he stuck matches in his beard and lighted them just before going into battle. He was such a scary sight, that the other pirate ships often surrendered rather than fight him, he was so scary."

"And one time," said Griffin, "he shot two of his own shipmates in the knees!"

"Why?" asked Alex.

"He said it was just to remind them of who he was," Griffin explained.

"Who could forget Blackbeard?" said Christina. "He was so big and so tall and so mean."

"What ever happened to him?" Grant asked.

"Ohhhhh," said Mimi. The lantern flickered as a wisp of breeze passed through the tent. "They laid a trap for him and when they caught off guard his ship in the sandbars, they shot him and stabbed him and decapitated him."

"You mean like your coffee?" Grant asked, confused.

Christina snickered "That's decaffeinated, Grant," she explained. "Decapitated means they cut off his head!"

Grant tucked his fists up under his chin and shivered in the lantern light. Their shadows wavered on the tent walls. Suddenly, the tent door flapped open. It was Uncle Joe. He looked as wild-eyed as any pirate.

"What is it?" Mimi asked.

Uncle Joe ignored her and glared at his tool bench. Mimi followed his gaze. Suddenly, they all realized what he was looking at—nothing! When they had come in, they had not noticed that his dark work bench was empty. All the tools had now disappeared. There was a rip in the screen in the window over the bench.

8
KILL DEVIL HILLS

The kids had been ordered to go to bed. Mimi and Uncle Joe hovered over his work bench, then went outside. Christina wondered where Papa was. Maybe he went to check on *My Girl*, she thought.

After lots of whispers and squirming, the other kids finally went to sleep. Christina pulled a small flashlight out of her backpack. She blew a layer of sand off the lens. Carefully, she made her pillow into a mound and pulled the blanket up over it and her head. She aimed the light on the small book she had found on Uncle Joe's reading table. She thought if she knew more about the Wright brothers' famous "first flight," she might be able to figure out why someone would steal the replica of their airplane. As the wind whined outside, she began to read:

Two Brothers, One Dream: "Let's Fly!"

*I*t is a cold winter's day. It is, in fact, December 17, 1903—a day that will go down in history. But brothers Orville and Wilbur Wright do not care about that at the moment.

*S*tanding on the gigantic sand dune called Kill Devil Hill in Kitty Hawk, North Carolina, the two brothers shiver in the icy wind. They traipse across the blowing sand to the Flyer, their flying machine. At least they are counting on it to fly
. . . this time.

*I*t is Orville's turn to fly the plane. He cranks up the engine of the rather rickety-looking contraption that to some, perhaps, appears more an overgrown toy crafted of fabric and sticks. Like two gentlemen bidding one another farewell on a journey, the brothers shake hands.

*O*rville stretches out face-down on the bottom wing. Wilbur holds the tip of the wing steady. One of their helpers from the nearby Life Saving Station releases the wire that holds Flyer to the frozen ground.

Instantly, Flyer begins to roll forward on its launching rail. Faster, faster, ever faster, until—EUREKA!—the craft is aloft . . . moving through the sky . . . heading into history. At last, at last success!

Christina closed the book and turned off her flashlight. She snuggled down into the blanket and closed her eyes tightly. It was a fascinating story, she thought, but it didn't really give her any clues as to why someone would steal the new *Flyer.*

Could it have blown away? Was it a prank? Was anyone mad at Uncle Joe? Surely the replica was valuable. Maybe someone stole it to sell on the Internet. Or to a museum. Or . . . . just . . . Christina was too sleepy to consider any other possibilities. For this night, the mystery of the missing plane would stay a mystery.

9

TWO BICYCLES BUILT FOR TWO

The next morning, the sun beamed brightly in the tent windows. It was warm and muggy again. Uncle Joe called it the "calm before the storm." He had put his weather radio on his work bench and it squelched its news in the background. He and Mimi were having coffee at the camp table.

Christina stretched and yawned. She loved mornings when she could stay all tucked into bed listening to birds and other morning sounds. But this morning, she heard no birds, and the talk back and forth between Uncle Joe and Mimi sounded discouraging.

Finally, she slid off her cot and wrapped her blanket around her and joined them at the table. Mimi poured her a glass of orange juice. There was a pile of fresh cinnamon rolls dripping with white frosting. Christina helped herself, munching quietly while she listened to the ongoing conversation.

"Big trouble," Uncle Joe said.

"Not much time to solve this mystery," said Mimi.

"How could security have been so lax?"

"It really wasn't. The guards were called to a false alarm just over the dune. It was a trick."

"What do your tools have to do with it?"

"How should I know?"

"The newspapers will hear about it. It will be awful publicity for the celebration."

"Where can the plane be? It's not like hiding a lunch box. It's big."

"Who would want it? What would they do with it? Makes no sense."

"No sense at all."

"Listen! Storm's coming. Gonna be a disaster."

"Don't say that."

Back and forth they mumbled to one another. Christina felt like she was eavesdropping in plain sight. They ignored her, but they couldn't ignore them all. For suddenly, the rest of the kids appeared fully dressed.

"Can we go bike riding?" Alex asked, grabbing a cinnamon roll.

Instead of the usual "third degree" about *where are you going and when will you be back and be careful and watch out for your brother*, etc., the distracted adults just nodded. Christina dashed for her clothes, dressed, and ran out of the tent. She shouted good morning to Papa as he passed her. He looked tired and angry. Quickly, she joined the other kids behind the tent where the bikes were parked.

The bicycles were beat-up beach bikes. There were only two, but each had two seats, one behind the other, and two sets of pedals. Whatever bright colors they had been painted originally were now faded to a scratched gray. The handle bars were rusty, but they had good tires, and except for some squeaking, they rode pretty well.

"You know, Orville and Wilbur had a bike shop," Alex said, as they rode along.

"I guess that's how they learned to be so handy with tools," Griffin said. "And later, motors."

"Didn't they go to school?" Grant asked, huffing and puffing as he pumped.

"Yeah," said Alex. "But they didn't like school as much as they liked experimenting on their own."

"Mimi says some kids learn better doing hands-on stuff instead of just sitting in a classroom," Christina said, pumping hard.

"That would be me," said Grant, sticking his skinny, little legs straight out, letting his sister do all the work.

"That's why I love field trips!" said Griffin.

"Yeah," said Alex. "Too bad they had this 100th anniversary during the holiday break."

Without another word, Griffin peeled off the paved road and their muscles burned as they rode the rest of the way uphill to the monument. When they got to the top, they stopped and walked around the awesome structure.

"This thing's a lot bigger up close than from down there," Grant said, motioning to the bottom of the dune which seemed very far away from up here.

Christina peered down at what looked like a busy little village below. Each day, there seemed to be more commotion. There were a lot of people in military uniforms. She guessed they were part of the official ceremonies that would be coming up in just a couple of days. Workmen were putting up tents for the souvenirs and food concessions. They could hear the, "Testing, testing, one, two, three," on the public address system.

"Hey!" shouted Grant. "Look over there!"

The kids all looked to where he pointed behind them on the dunes that rolled in waves down to the sound. Colorful hang gliders were soaring from the top of Jockey's Ridge almost down to the water.

Behind the dunes was a small village of ramshackle beach houses. There were junk cars parked in the yards. Here, the dunes fizzled out into the windblown **maritime** forest. Christina wondered who lived down there.

"And look over there!" cried Griffin. He pointed in a different direction, out past the museum building and the tents to the large open area where the air show was going to take place. Little bi-planes, big helicopters, and many other types of aircraft were parked. People in jumpsuits bustled around each plane.

Christina squinted to see if she saw *Flyer* anywhere, but she didn't. Suddenly, what she did see from their perch on top of the highest dune was a string of police cars flashing blue lights coming down the highway. To her surprise, they turned into the park. They wound slowly around the road until they came to Uncle Joe's tent—where they stopped.

"Come on, you guys!" she said, hopping on her bike. "Something's happening down there! Let's go!"

10

JUST SEND MY MAIL TO THE MANTEO JAIL

Christina sped off quickly with her brother behind her, sand tugging at the tires. Soon she was on the pavement again, rolling down the hill as fast as she dared. She turned once to see if Alex and Griffin were behind her and keeping up. They all skidded to a stop in front of the tent just in time to see the police handcuffing Papa!

Christina thought she would cry. "What are they doing?" she begged Mimi.

Uncle Joe was pleading with the police. He slammed his fist into his palm angrily when they would not listen. Mimi looked very worried. She put Papa's jacket around his shoulders and scowled at the police officers.

"We're just doing our job, ma'am," the officer insisted.

"And what job is that?" Mimi demanded.

"Hush, puppy," Papa said gently. "We'll get this straightened out," he promised, but he did not look too sure.

As the officer placed Papa's hands behind his back and put a pair of handcuffs around them, he said, "You are under arrest for the theft of the replica First Flight aircraft known as *Flyer*."

Christina and the other kids gasped. Mimi got out her cell phone and started dialing. Uncle Joe slammed into the tent. As the officer put Papa in the back seat of his patrol car, Papa winked at Christina. But she could see that he looked tired and scared. Surely, this was turning out to be the awfulest trip they had ever taken. As the patrol car pulled away and Christina looked to see all the people standing around staring at them like they were criminals, she began to cry. So did Grant.

Inside the tent, around the table, Mimi tried to explain. "They think Papa stole *Flyer*."

"But why would they think that?" Christina cried.

"Because they found out that his tools from *My Girl* were the ones used to break into this tent," said Uncle Joe.

"If Papa took *Flyer*, what do they think he did with the plane?" Grant asked. "Eat it?"

In spite of themselves, they laughed.

"Let's just stay calm," said Mimi, who did not look calm at all. "Uncle Joe and I have to follow Papa into town. We will get him out on bail. I'll get a lawyer. It'll be alright, you'll see," she reassured the children. But she did not sound like she believed that.

Christina slammed her fist down on the table. "Well, it's just a stupid old pretend airplane," she said. "It's not even the real thing. So how serious can this be?" From the way she saw Uncle Joe and Mimi look at one another, she understood that it was as serious as could be. It made her want to cry again.

"Listen," said Mimi, grabbing her purse. "You kids just hang out here. Go over and look around the museum. Here's some money. Get a hot dog or something. Uncle Joe and I will be back as quickly as we can." She gave Christina her look that meant *please cooperate*.

Christina ran and gave her grandmother a hug. "We will, Mimi," she said. "I promise. Just go bring Papa back. Fast!"

Mimi sighed in relief. She gave a sad little smile. "Yes! Gotta get Papa. Gotta go to the Ball!" She looked like she would cry, but instead, she hugged all the kids in a great giant group hug and dashed out of the tent to the car. Uncle Joe shook his finger at them as if to say *be good*, then followed her.

As soon as they left, the kids started to go to the museum as they had promised. As the last one out, Christina secured the tent flap as best she could against the fussy wind. Uncle Joe's radio was still on. She heard the forecaster say, "Dare County is now under a hurricane warning." They were in Dare County. She decided not to tell the other kids.

At the museum building, Alex flashed her special card that let them inside since her Dad was one of the official airplane mechanics. At first, the kids were fidgety. It was hard to settle down and have fun when they were so worried and the wind was blowing so hard outside. But in here, like in most museums, things were calm and quiet. Soon, the kids were captivated by the exhibits on display and began to wander around trying to look at everything at once.

Christina stopped and looked at the display about wing warping. It told how Orville and Wilbur had had to figure out the science of flying. They practiced with kites—not just flying them, but keeping them under control. This gave them the

Alex and the Wright Brothers

idea that a glider could fly for a longer time if a pilot was actually flying the airplane.

And then, they had one of those "Eureka!" moments. The brothers knew that when air moved over a wing that was "warped" (curved at the top), that it provided "lift" to the wing. That made them suspect that perhaps a pilot could control the lift of an aircraft. Especially if the plane had a motor!

Grant read the information aloud to himself. As he read, he spread his arms into arcs, creating a warped wing. "Eureka!" he cried suddenly. "I think I've got it!"

Christina laughed at her brother and patted him on the head. "Good job, Grant!" she said. "I think you'll make a good inventor one day." She and Grant loved to watch those shows on TV where people took a mishmash of junkyard stuff and created a robot or something else neat and cool.

But it was difficult for Christina to enjoy much of the exhibit. She was antsy in her pantsy, as Mimi always put it. She knew Mimi and Uncle Joe would take care of Papa and get him out of jail, but what if they didn't? What if the police thought they had enough proof to convict him on charges of stealing something as important as the 100th anniversary replica of the Wright Brothers' airplane? The plane that was supposed to re-enact the First Flight (Christina looked at her Carole Marsh Mystery watch) in less than 48 hours!

She waited near the entrance to the gift shop for the other kids to finish their tour. She overheard two people in the shop talking to one another.

"Yeah," the first person said. "That guy's gonna be in some kind of trouble. Why would he steal the plane? What would he do with it? It sure can't go very far."

"Aw, it's probably in a million pieces now," said the second person. "He must be a real jerk—probably just some nut who's mad at the world. They'll never find that plane before the celebration, that's for sure."

Christina couldn't stand it any longer. "Alex! Grant! Griffin! Get over here." The kids ran to join her.

"What is it?" Grant asked. "Time for lunch?" he added, hopefully.

"No!" said Christina, stomping her foot. "It's time for us to take control of the situation. We're going to find that airplane. *Now!*"

11

HOT DOG

Christina was outvoted. Not about searching for the airplane. But first, the other kids insisted, they just had to have something to eat. Reluctantly, Christina agreed; she was starving, too.

At the snack bar, they ordered hot dogs and chocolate shakes. Outside the window, the wind seemed to be blowing harder. Christina noticed that most folks wore jackets and ducked into the wind as they walked, pulling their hats down to avoid getting the blowing sand into their eyes. She wondered what the weather radio was forecasting now.

"And how are we going to find *Flyer*?" Alex asked.

"We only have one hope," Christina explained. "The plane's pretty big, so perhaps it's somewhere nearby, only hidden."

"But what if someone took it all apart?" Griffin asked.

Christina sighed. "That's why I said we only have one chance. If someone took the plane apart, we'll never find it."

Grant looked puzzled. "But where is *nearby*?" he asked.

Griffin snapped his fingers. "I know," he said. "Finish your lunch, and I'll show you!"

As soon as everyone had gobbled down the rest of their lunch and wiped the ketchup and chocolate from their faces, they followed Griffin back into the museum. He ran directly to a large map on the wall. "See!" he said. "Here's an aerial view of Wright Brothers National Memorial . . . and some of the surrounding land and water."

Christina stood on her tiptoes to examine the map more closely. "I guess this is our search area," she agreed.

"Mimi said the sand ate up stuff sometimes," Grant reminded them. "Maybe it ate up *Flyer*."

Christina shook her head. "I think Mimi meant over a long time, not overnight," she said to her brother. But it did make her wonder if someone could have moved the plane and covered it with sand. It would have certainly made the airplane "invisible"—so that it was there, but not really there. She looked at the endless rolling dunes on the map. If that's what had happened, she thought, it would be like finding a needle in a haystack.

"Could someone have flown it off and it crashed into the Croatan Sound?" Alex asked.

"Uncle Joe didn't think just anyone could fly it," Griffin reminded her. "Besides, surely someone would have seen a 100-year-old airplane gliding through the sky!"

"That's what folks from all over the world are coming here to see soon," Christina said. "And we have to see that they do!"

"Maybe we could get up high and look around," Grant suggested. "Like back on top of the big sand dune where the monument is. Where we rode our bikes this morning."

"Hey!" Christina said. "You're right, Grant!" Her brother beamed; he liked to be right. "We do need to get up HIGH and see what we can see."

Griffin thought he got her drift. "You mean like really high?"

"Yeah!" Christina said with a smile. Now Alex smiled; she understood, too.

"What do you mean?" Grant asked, confused.

"C'mon," his sister said. "And we'll show you!"

They fled out of the museum and hopped on their bikes. They had to pump hard to make any headway against the wind. When they got to the tent, they ran inside to get jackets and caps. Christina stopped long enough to listen to the weather radio:

CRACKLE degrees longitude SQUELCH and 35 degrees CRACKLE latitude SQUELCH winds at 79 miles per hour and rising . . . small craft advisory in effect for . . .

"What's it say?" Alex asked as she zipped up.

"Well, I didn't hear the word hurricane, at least," Christina said, slapping her cap on her head.

The kids dashed out of the tent. They were on their bikes and had headed off, so they did not hear the radio when this broadcast came:

SQUELCH CRACKLE hurricane warnings now in effect for all of Dare County, northern Virginia, the Outer Banks, south to Cape Hatteras CRACKLE residents should take precautions SQUELCH evacuation now underway CRACKLE bridges will be closed when winds reach 45 miles per hour SQUELCH CRACKLE warning SQUELCH CRACKLE SQUELCH warning warning

12

HANGING BY A THREAD

They rode back up the hill and past the monument. The memorial road ended. The kids thought they could surf their bikes down the backside of the dunes, but that didn't work. The soft sand sucked the wheels and spokes down until they could no longer pedal.

They abandoned the useless bikes. Christina looked ahead. The dunes seemed to roll on forever. We could be in the middle of the Sahara Desert, she thought to herself. Timbuctu could be right over the ridge. Then she reminded herself to quit daydreaming and come up with a search plan. "Follow me!" she said, spitting sand.

Onward they trudged. At first they tried to talk, but walking against the wind, it was just too difficult. It seemed like they had been climbing for hours. It was hard to tell because there was no sun. In fact, the sky, the water, and the sand all had the same sickly gray appearance.

Suddenly, Christina pointed ahead to the top of a small dune. Perched on top was a lime green hang glider. No one seemed to be around. In fact, no one seemed to be on Jockey's Ridge at all today. Once more, she pointed and spit sand as she cried to the others, "Head for that dune!"

By the time they reached the top of the dune, they were exhausted. They had had to grab Grant by the arms and lug him up the last part of the hill. They all fell onto the sand, then huddled up beneath the long wings of the hang glider.

"Think we could borrow this thing for a little while?" Christina asked.

"Think we could all go to jail with your Papa for stealing airplanes?" Alex retorted.

Christina was angry. "My Papa did not steal an airplane!" she said. "Besides, I said *borrow*."

"We don't know how to fly it," said Grant.

"I've never flown one," Griffin admitted. "But me and Alex have been up in one with Dad before."

Look at those storm clouds!

"How hard can it be?" Christina said. "Tourists come here and pay their money and fly these things all the time."

Alex peered up at the winged contraption. "Yeah, but they get lessons . . . and safety gear."

Christina was undaunted. She knew this was not smart. It was not brave. It was dumb. But she was determined. "Anyone who wants to go back, can," she said. "Everyone else—grab hold!"

One by one, they grabbed on to the hang glider. "We'll never get this thing off the ground with all this weight," Griffin said.

For awhile, they perched on the dune, clinging to the hang glider's frame. Then, just when they were least expecting it, a gust of wind caused the glider's wings to tilt left, then right. The nose tilted forward, then backward. Just when they were each about to let go, the hang glider took off.

First it rose up into the air just a little, as if taking a deep breath. When it touched back down, it was with a soft clunk onto the sand. Each child let out a breathless little squeal.

Warp, Christina said to herself. *Warp* and *lift*. Orville could do it. Wilbur could do it. So can we. At least a little ways. The hang glider tipped to port, then starboard, and suddenly they were airborne.

"Heeeeeeeeeeeeey!" said Grant. "We're flying!"

"Hold on tight!" Christina warned her little brother. She did not feel so brave now. In fact, she was afraid for their lives.

"We have no control!" said Alex.

"Sure we do," Griffin insisted. "He shifted his weight and the aircraft responded.

Suddenly, they were off the dune and rising across the sand at the mercy of the wind. It was clear to them now—way too late—that no one had been using the hang glider today because it was just too windy. You need wind to fly, Christina thought, but not so much wind. Not too much wind. Not this wind!

In spite of the wind, the hang glider sailed smoothly along. The kids had one brief scare as the glider appeared to be headed out over the sound. Christina was certain they did not want to crash there—not without life preservers. Then she wished she had not thought of the term—crash land. But Griffin shifted his weight and the other kids followed suit and the craft veered back in the right direction.

For a few minutes, it all seemed like fun. The breeze was cold, but invigorating. Christina got down to business. "Griffin," she ordered, "keep us steered over the memorial area so we can look for *Flyer*."

"I'll try," Griffin yelled back at her. It was difficult to hear in the wind. "But this is not a real airplane you know. It doesn't have any power."

"Well, do the best you can," Christina begged him. "We can only make one pass, so keep a sharp eye out for anything that looks like an airplane hidden in bushes, or behind a dune, or, well, I don't know where, but keep looking!"

The kids did just that as the hang glider swerved and dipped, rose and dove, but mostly stayed on a course over the wide area of the Wright Brothers National Memorial. Mostly, they just saw sand. All the people who had been out and about earlier were nowhere to be seen.

Christina looked all around. Except for the buildings, there was little to see except for the maritime forest which surrounded the site.

The woods were made up of low, gnarled, windblown yaupon trees and other shrubs. It was impossible to see beneath the knotted groves.

"Over there!" Christina hollered to Griffin, who nodded, and responded. The hang glider reacted to his movement, and they spiraled over the small village near the sound. Christina spotted a few rundown cottages, a wrecked dune buggy. A rusted Jeep stopped in front of one of the cottages. The car doors flew open and three women tumbled out. They ducked and headed for their cottage.

"What's that?" Alex asked. She nodded to a windmill swirling in the wind. It was directly below them and seemed to belong to the women's cottage.

"Just an old windmill," Christina said. "They were once common on the Outer Banks. People used them for a power source. Papa told me."

"Then how come I've never seen one before?" Alex demanded.

"I don't know," Christina said. "Maybe it's a replica." She didn't see what difference it made. It wasn't *Flyer*, she thought. In fact, they had not spied anything out of the ordinary.

Suddenly, Grant screamed. He had lost hold with one hand, and was swinging—trapeze artist style—by his white-knuckled other hand from the hang glider.

"Hold on!" Christina pleaded. She reached out and grabbed his loose arm, and fighting the wind, placed it back on the glider.

It was a good thing they were all holding on, because the glider took a sudden swoop upward.

They all screamed. Christina just knew that the glider was going to spin them upside down. The glider seemed to have a mind of its own. As if it had a plan, it dove gently toward the sand and skidded so closely over the dune nearest the maritime forest that the kids' feet drug the ground.

"Hold on!" yelled Alex.

"Get ready to let go!" shouted Griffin.

"We're coming in for a . . ." Christina began.

"LANDING!" Grant squealed.

13

THE WITCHES' COTTAGE

The hang glider thudded to a stop so close to one of the cottages, that it caused the three women to turn around and glare at the kids with shocked stares.

The kids let loose of the glider and tumbled every which way. Christina didn't know whether to laugh or cry. They were safe. But they had failed. Oh, well, she thought. Orville and Wilbur had failed before they succeeded, she remembered. Only she didn't have much time left to succeed.

At least no one was hurt. Grant, who had fallen on his tummy, picked his face up out of the sand and blew. He looked up at the women staring at him. "Hi!" he said.

The oldest woman glared at him. "No trespassing!" she said, in a very ugly tone of voice.

The kids struggled up from the sand and dusted themselves off. The women—looking like three ugly witches in some fairytale to Christina—continued to stare at the kids, as if they wished they could make them vanish.

"Who are you? What are you doing here? And when are you going to leave?" growled the youngest woman.

"Do you have a telephone?" Christina asked.

"No!" the middle woman said.

"Could we have some water?" Grant asked, scraping sand from his tongue.

"Forget it!" said the oldest woman.

"Well, can we come inside?" Alex asked. She looked exhausted. "I have to go to the bathroom."

"Tough!" said women all together.

Then, the three women put their messy-haired heads together and whispered to one another. Suddenly, they completely changed their attitude.

"Just kidding," said the youngest woman, with a fake smile. "Come inside and clean up. I have a cell phone and you can call your parents to come and get you."

The women lead the way up the rickety steps. They let the tattered screen door slam behind them.

Christina felt like they were about to enter the wicked witch's house from *Hansel and Gretel*. But she didn't know what else to do. Maybe if they could just make a quick phone call, they could get out of here. They'd be in trouble with Mimi, Papa, and Uncle Joe, but anywhere seemed better than here at the moment, especially with the weather getting worse all the time.

As the kids headed for the cottage, they suddenly bolted backwards, as the ugliest of the women threw the screen door open. "Get in here!" she screamed.

When the children refused, the women huddled to talk among themselves once more. Never saying a word, they motioned for the kids to get in their rusty Jeep. They drove them almost all the way up the hill to the monument, then made them get out. Without saying goodbye or good luck, or get lost, or anything, they sped back down the hill toward their creepy cottage.

"Let's go!" Christina encouraged them. It seemed like a long walk back to the tent, but at least it was all downhill. The flapping wind and the scudding sand were irritating. It was also getting colder.

Christina was surprised that there were no people around. She knew there must still be lots to do to get ready for the celebration. Surely the weather would break and they would be back to their chores soon. But right now, she just couldn't think about that. She had hoped to see Papa's car parked in front of the tent, but it was not there. Neither was Uncle Joe's Jeep.

The kids scrambled inside the tent and took off their jackets, sand spewing everywhere. "I'll sweep it up later," Alex said, wearily.

Christina went directly to the galley and began to make peanut butter and jelly sandwiches. The bread was a little moldy, but no one seemed to care. The weather radio made a horrible screeching sound, so Christina turned it down. She glanced at the clock on Uncle Joe's work bench and was surprised to see that it was already five o'clock. Here on the far east coast it was already getting dark, especially since it was just a few days from the winter solstice, the shortest day of the year.

The kids sat down and ate their sandwiches off paper towels. Griffin poured them each a paper cup of milk. They ate without speaking. Then they went and climbed on their cots to take a nap.

"We didn't accomplish much, did we?" Christina said to the ceiling.

"Well, we didn't find *Flyer*, if that's what you mean," Alex said.

"We'll look some more, as soon as we rest," Griffin promised.

"I wish we had TV," Grant said. "I really like that junkyard show, where kids make stuff out of stuff."

Christina laughed. "You like all TV," she said. But Grant did not answer; he was already asleep, little specks of sand shining on his pink cheeks.

Just after Christina fell asleep, the weather radio come back to life. It was in the middle of a forecast:

SCREECH SQUELCH Dare County has been evacuated. All bridges are now closed. The next hurricane update will come in two minutes—stay tuned. CRACKLE SQUELCH.

14

NO DREAM

As the children slept, the storm—now at full force hurricane strength—bore down on the coast. The enormous monster reached from the sea to the sky. In the very center of the storm was the eye. The eye was calm, but not peaceful. For all around the eye was a swirling tube of angry gray cloud.

Out on the sea, the hurricane spawned waterspouts—tornadoes made of water. They popped out of the giant clouds and sped across the top of the water like an out of control animal. While they did no harm out on the water, once the storm came ashore, they could tear apart anything on land.

All across North Carolina, from Virginia to the north to the South Carolina border, everyone was boarded up. The beaches had been evacuated. The bridges were closed. Only a few "old salts" who had weathered hurricanes before stayed put. A winter hurricane was unusual, but not unheard of. A winter hurricane was especially frightening because of the cold, icy wind and water it thundered down. The danger was the wind . . . and the storm surge that could flood low-lying areas.

As the early winter dark settled down upon Kill Devil Hills, only four people remained at the famous Wright Brothers National Memorial: Christina, Grant, Alex, and Griffin.

Christina was the first to awaken. She immediately knew something was wrong. No, she thought to herself, stretching beneath the scratchy army blanket. Nothing's wrong. Everything is better. The wind had died down. Why it's as quiet as a mouse outside, she marveled.

Of course, everything isn't alright, she thought. Mimi and Papa and Uncle Joe still had not come back. This was not like them at all. They had not even called. Where were they? Where was everyone else, in fact? Christina felt a lump in her throat and a knot in the pit of her stomach. Her instincts told her something was wrong. Bad wrong, Really bad wrong. Maybe it was the quiet.

Soon, all the other kids stirred. They were dirty and sandy and tired and hungry. They were scared.

Christina struggled off her cot. It was very chilly inside the tent. White frost glistened the sides of the tent. Wrapped in the army blanket, she went to the work bench and jiggled the weather radio:

SQUELCH CRACKLE SCREECH

Rubbing her eyes, she went to the tent door and opened the flap. It was dark. The moon and stars shown overhead. In fact, the moon hung low over the monument on the hill and seem to illuminate it. The stars twinkled like diamond chips. It was beautiful.

"Come look!" she whispered to the others. Wrapped in their own blankets, they came up behind Christina and peered outside. Soon, they were all outdoors. The wind was quiet. There was not a sound to be heard. It was very eerie. And then, suddenly, they saw something they could not believe: SNOW.

"Snow!" cried Grant, lifting his little face up to the sky.

"At the beach!" Alex marveled.

"In winter," said Griffin. He stuck out his tongue, trying to catch the free-falling flakes.

"It's like Christmas!" said Christina. "A magical, wonderful Christmas."

They all began to move forward out onto the sand, laughing and catching snowflakes. It was like being in their own special ballet. It felt like now and it felt like it could be a hundred years ago. Just the sand and the stars and the sound of children laughing.

But suddenly, the snow turned to icy needles. "Hey, it's changed to sleet!" Griffin said.

"Ouch!" cried Grant, pulling his blanket over his head.

Even on the soft sand the icy pellets made a *ticking* sound as they fell. Soon the pellets were the size of quarters. Alex rubbed her head. "It hurts!"

"Quick!" said Christina, "run for the tent."

Stumbling on the sand, it was slow going with the blankets tripping them up or trailing behind them. Their bare feet hurt from the hard ice balls.

Before they could reach the tent, the wind began to blow. Christina looked up just in time to see the moon and stars disappear. A cold chill that had nothing to do with the night air or the sleet roamed over her body. She had the strangest feeling that she now understood what was wrong. Very, very wrong.

Quickly, she shoved the kids back inside the tent. They had to fight to get it zipped up, the wind was now blowing so fiercely. As the kids threw off their blankets and dashed to put on dry clothing, the radio crackled back to life. It was just as Christina had suspected.

SCREECH CRACKLE The National Weather Service reports the eye of the hurricane now situated over CRACKLE SCREECH Kill Devil Hills. SQUELCH CRACKLE

The children gasped. "A hurricane?" said Grant. "Here? Now?" He looked scared to death.

"How could that happen?" Christina asked, incredulous that they had found themselves in this dangerous situation.

Griffin's teeth chattered as he spoke. "Don't you remember? Uncle Joe said there might be a hurricane."

"Yeah," said Alex. "Sometime. Somewhere. But not here, not now."

From the roar outside the tent, it was clear that the hurricane *was* here, *now*. Once more the radio blared:

The eye of the hurricane SQUELCH passed over Kill Devil Hills at 6:15 p.m. SCREECH The back side of this serious storm is now passing over Kitty Hawk. SCREECH

"Well, that's for sure!" said Griffin. The wind outside was growing louder and louder. The tent shivered and shook.

"How long can it last?" Alex asked.

"I don't know," said Christina. "I guess the first part of the storm passed over while we were asleep. But I always heard that the back side of a hurricane was the worst side."

"Worse?" Grant asked, wide-eyed.

Outside, the furious wind swirled around the tent as if determined to get inside. Christina grabbed the phone to call 911. The phone was dead. She looked over on the work bench. Uncle Joe's cell phone was there. Christina tried it. There was no dial tone. There was no way to call for help.

"Where is Uncle Joe?" Griffin pleaded.

"Yeah," said Grant, "where are Mimi and Papa? They wouldn't leave us out in a storm like this."

Christina agreed. "Maybe they couldn't get back. Maybe the bridges were closed, or the road was flooded."

"I'll bet they've been trying to call," lamented Alex. "I'll bet they're as worried about us as . . . as . . . as we are worried about *us*. Are we safe in here?"

Suddenly, the tent walls began to mash inward. Overhead the top of the tent seemed to reach down and grab at their heads. The work bench trembled. Sand scudded in beneath the bottom of the tent. The dishes in the little wooded cupboard rattled.

"No!" said Christina. "We are *not* safe in here!"

And then, the lights went out. It was pitch black and the wind was as loud as a freight train.

"Let's get out of here!" Christina screamed.

15

ABANDON SHIP!

Without grabbing jackets or flashlights or anything else, the four children dashed out of the tent. Lightning stabbed the sky overhead. Sand blew into their faces, stinging their skin and eyes, forcing its way into their mouths. With the heavy sheets of rain, visibility was zero. When a bolt of lighting lit up the sky, Christina pointed toward the museum. "Head over there!"

Holding hands to try to stay together, they bent their heads into the wind and made a mad dash for the museum. Sometimes they could see the sand-colored structure; other times, they could not. Sometimes the wind blew them forward toward the structure. Other times, it shoved them back toward the tent. They heard a loud rumble behind them and turned to see the tent explode into a million splintery pieces.

"RUN!" Christina screamed. "RUN!"

The kids ran as fast as the wind and rain and ankle-grabbing sand would let them. Beneath another bright bolt of lightning, they hurdled the last few yards toward the museum. The door was locked. Instead, they burrowed into a small hallway between the museum and the restrooms. They drew themselves into a tight huddle and closed their eyes against the mighty and fearful storm.

"Help!" Grant cried. "Please!"

Christina looked down at her brother, smothered beneath her.

"Are you hurt?" she screamed above the wind.

"Yes!" Grant yelled back. His face was pinched with pain.

"Where" his sister demanded.

"My arm," Grant said with a whimper.

"How is it hurt?" pleaded Christina.

Grant gave her a desperate look. "It's you. You still have such a tight hold on it, it's killing me. Let go, please!"

In relief, Christina pried her fingers off her brother's arm. Her fingerprints were mashed into his skin.

"Sorry, Grant," she said.

"It's ok," he told her. "I'm glad you held on to me."

With a great relief, the kids realized that the furious storm was abating. It was still raining cats and dogs (and even a few frogs!), but at least it wasn't raining sideways now. The wind had calmed down so that they could even talk without screaming at one another. The lightning bolts were fewer, and the thunder was less rumbly.

"I think we made it," Griffin said. "I really do."

"Thank goodness," said Alex. "That was perfectly awful!"

"Now what?" said Grant. He looked wistfully at the place where the tent had once stood.

"I don't know," Christina admitted. She had never felt so lost or alone—even with the other kids here.

Suddenly, a bolt of lightning seemed to strike right into the tunnel where they hovered. The kids screamed. But it wasn't lightning. It was headlights. The headlights of a vehicle. A wet, hooded figure got out of the car. With the bright light in their faces, the children could not see if the person had come to help or hurt them. Christina thought of the angry women.

When the figure reached them, a hand pulled up a hood over its face and there stood Papa. "Thank goodness!" he cried. He grabbed the children into his arms.

Mimi and Uncle Joe bounded out of the car. Mimi had an umbrella but the wind blew it inside out and she tossed it away. She ran toward the children. "Oh, am I glad to see you!" she said. Tears were streaming down her face. She hugged and kissed each of them.

Uncle Joe dashed up the steps and wrapped a big, blue tarp around the kids to keep the wind and rain off of them. He gave the kids a hug. "What did you guys do with my tent?"

"Oh, Dad," Griffin began, "we didn't do it, I promise!"

In spite of themselves, the adults laughed. "I was kidding, Griffin," he assured his son. "I was kidding."

"Where have you been?" Christina asked them.

"We got trapped in Manteo," Papa said. "They closed the bridges. We called and called. Where were you kids?"

The kids did not answer. How could they admit that they had been out hang gliding and looking for *Flyer* in a hurricane, Christina thought.

But Mimi saved the day by saying, "The wind is dying down. Let's get into the car. We've got to get these kids dry before they catch their death of cold."

"Please don't say *death*, Mimi," Grant said. Mimi scooped him up and headed for the car. Papa followed with both girls in his arms. Uncle Joe tucked Griffin beneath his arm like a football and dashed for the car too.

Inside the car, Papa turned on the heater and the defroster. Their warm breath was turning the cold windows so foggy that they couldn't see out of them. That didn't stop Papa. He put the car into gear and spun it around in the sand.

As they found the paved road and slowly crept out of the flooded memorial site to the highway, Christina glanced out of the now clear windows. There was one more spatter of lightning. She looked up toward the monument and saw the dark silhouette of three women.

16

A MOTEL IS A WONDERFUL THING

"A motel is a wonderful thing!" said Mimi. They were camped out in a small motel that had re-opened. The owner was an oldtimer who had stayed to "weather the storm."

Since the motel had a generator, they were able to take hot showers and dry their hopelessly tangled hair. One by one, the kids curled up on the king-sized bed like bunnies, in their tightly twisted towels.

Papa and Uncle Joe said they were going out to find "room service." That made the kids laugh, but they were hopeful. Soon, the men returned with a large pepperoni pizza, steaming hot.

"Where in the world did you get that?" Mimi asked, amazed.

"You just gotta know where to go," Uncle Joe said with a laugh.

They put the pizza on the little round table and gathered round to eat slices of what Christina was certain had to be the most delicious pizza ever made. Just as she was getting comfortable, the questions that she feared began.

"So where *were* you kids this afternoon?" Uncle Joe asked.

"We called and we called," said Mimi.

"We finally sent the security guards to look after you," Papa added. "They told us they would get you off the island before the hurricane hit. We never knew they couldn't find you. Where were you?"

The kids glanced at one another nervously. The adults waited patiently for some explanation. Rain still spattered outside, but it was clear the storm was over and they were out of danger—except from the possible wrath of the adults.

Finally, Christina bravely began. "We went to the museum first," she said.

"We even had lunch there," Alex added.

"They have really, really good hot dogs," Grant volunteered.

"I don't think that's what they want to know," Griffin said, grimly. He put down his pizza. So did the rest of the kids.

Christina let out a big sigh and began to explain the unexplainable. "We were worried about you, Papa! We thought if we could find *Flyer*, we could prove you had nothing to do with its disappearance. Then, Mimi could get you out of jail and clear your name."

Papa looked weepy. "I know you care, Christina," he said. "But I was ok. I never went to jail. We went to the courthouse and handled it all for now. You need to let adults handle adult matters."

Christina nodded. But the questioning was not over.

"You looked for *Flyer*?" Mimi said. "How did you think you could find it?"

"We had some help," Grant volunteered before the other kids could shush him up.

"What kind of help?" asked Mimi.

For a minute the kids said nothing. The pizza sat there getting cold. Rain pelted the windows.

"Help?" Mimi repeated.

Griffin gave in first. "A hang glider," he told them.

"And where did you get a hang glider?" asked Mimi. She had a frown on her face. Her frown had tomato sauce on top of it, but the kids didn't even laugh.

"We borrowed it," said Grant.

"To do what?" Mimi asked.

Christina decided that it had been her idea so she'd better explain. "We thought we could fly it over the dunes and if *Flyer* had been moved or hidden, we might spot it." She hushed and waited for the adults to yell at her.

Mimi glared at them beneath her furrowed brow. "You mean to tell me that you borrowed a hang glider and the four of you thought you'd hang on to it and fly it over the sand?"

Grant rushed right in. "We didn't think it, Mimi, we did it!" he said proudly.

Mimi groaned.

"You flew it over the dunes?" Papa asked, incredulous at the idea of four children suspended in the air from something as flimsy and uncontrollable as a hang glider.

"Yes," the four children admitted together.

Now it was Uncle Joe's turn. "And what about the hurricane?"

"We didn't know," Alex said, giving her three-fingered Girl Scout promise. "We were outdoors and the radio was acting up when we got back. We didn't know the storm was so bad until . . ."
She did not finish her sentence.

"Until what?" Mimi asked, in suspicion.

It was Griffin's turn to put his foot in his mouth. "Until we got back and took a nap and woke up and then we heard there was a hurricane."

The three adults stared at the children. Their mouths hung open as if they had been told the tallest tale on earth.

"And then what happened?" Mimi finally asked.

"We ran!" said Griffin.

"Fast!" said Alex. "To the museum—for cover."

Mimi shook her head. "And then what?"

The children looked at one another, puzzled.

"And then you came and got us?" Christina said. "And we were really, really, really glad!"

"Uh, and what about the tent?" Uncle Joe asked.

Together the kids proclaimed, "It blew down!"

"We didn't do it, I promise," Grant said.

To the surprise of all the children, the adults began to laugh. They laughed so hard that tears rolled down their faces. Mimi actually rolled around on the bed, holding her stomach she laughed so hard.

The kids looked at one another in amazement.

"And what's so funny?" Christina asked.

Mimi sat up and wiped tears from her cheeks. "Nothing's funny, Christina. We're just so relieved that you all are all right! You can't imagine how afraid we were for your safety. All this time, we think security has you and here you crazy kids are out flying a hang glider around in a hurricane. It's so wild and crazy it should be in a book!"

The kids felt a great deal of relief. Relief that they were safe. And relief that they were not really in any serious trouble. Slowly, they began to munch once more on the pizza. Until Uncle Joe asked in a funny voice, "And did you find *Flyer*?"

17

QUESTIONS AND ANSWERS

The four kids looked forlorn.

"No. No, we didn't," Christina finally admitted.

Uncle Joe looked at the children quizzically. "Where did you think you would find the plane?"

"We thought maybe it was buried in the sand," Griffin said. "And we might see its outline if we could get up above the dunes."

Uncle Joe smiled at his son. "You know, that's really smart thinking. Someone *could* have buried the plane like that—that would explain why it vanished so quickly with no one seeing any truck or anyone haul it off."

"Did you see anything suspicious?" asked Papa.

The kids were surprised that the adults were asking them all these questions. Had they been right? Were the dunes all around the memorial site the best place to search? If so, why hadn't they found the plane?

"We met some ugly, old ladies," Grant said.

"In the old village by the sound," Alex added.

"There's a windmill over there," said Griffin.

Uncle Joe looked puzzled. "No there isn't," he said with a laugh. "You kids must have been seeing things."

"No," said Christina. "There really is a windmill. And their ugly, old cottage. Who lives over there, anyway?"

"Oh, just the **descendants** of some older Outer Banks families. They are sort of strange, but they don't cause any harm. I don't recall three unattractive women, though."

"What did they do to you?" Mimi asked.

"They just brought us back to the top of the hill," said Christina.

"Not all the way back to the tent or the museum?" Papa asked.

"No," said Alex. "I don't really think they wanted anyone to see them."

"Why would that be?" Joe puzzled.

"Cause they are so UGLY!" Grant insisted.

The kids laughed, but Mimi frowned at them. "That really isn't very nice, you know."

"We know," said Christina, "but they really were ugly and they really were hateful. And they dumped us out in the middle of a hurricane."

"That's true," Mimi agreed. She looked like she'd like to get her hands on the women and give them a piece of her mind about how they had treated the kids.

Now, it was the kids' turn to ask the questions.

"What did they say at the jail?" Christina asked.

Papa frowned. "They said *My Girl* had been broken into. Someone stole my tool box."

"So they thought you stole your own tools?" Griffin asked, confused.

"No," said Papa. "Later, they found the tool box and it had Uncle Joe's tools in it—with my fingerprints all over them."

"But you and Uncle Joe were at the work bench the other day. Of course, your fingerprints would have been on them," Christina said.

"I know, I know!" said Papa. "But somehow, the police think the tools have something to do with the theft of *Flyer*. And since I was from out of town and a stranger here . . . and they found my prints, they just came to the conclusion that I was a good suspect."

"Are you off the hook for now?" Christina asked.

"At least until they find whoever stole *Flyer*," Papa said, with a sigh.

Christina didn't like the sound of that. That didn't sound like being off the hook at all.

The sky was growing lighter. It was almost morning and the kids had not slept at all. Mimi insisted they climb up on the bed and take a nap. Uncle Joe had to get to the memorial site and check on the damage to the tent. Papa was going to help him. They said the celebration was still going on— *Flyer* or no *Flyer*. Mimi said she'd go out and bring them some breakfast—IF they promised not to leave the room, or fly any hang gliders, or visit any strange women.

"We promise!" the kids said together.

They slept for awhile, but soon, Grant woke up and turned on the TV. His favorite make-stuff-out-of-junk show was on. In spite of themselves, the rest of the sleepy children woke up and watched as well. They were happy to see Mimi when she returned with bags of fast food hotcakes and orange juice. She dished out the breakfast, then turned to leave again.

"Where are you going, Mimi?" Christina asked. She did not want all the adults to leave them alone again.

"I'll be right back," Mimi promised. "I've got to pick up my ball gown I dropped off at the cleaners—if it didn't blow away!" she said. "Tonight's the big ball, you know!" And then she left.

Christina knew she shouldn't, but she couldn't get *Flyer* off her mind. I'm like Orville and Wilbur, she thought to herself. They failed, but they kept trying until they finally succeeded. She wanted to keep trying, only she didn't have any idea where to begin. Was she really at a dead end? She refused to believe so. What she needed was a CLUE!

18

THE BALL

But there was no time for clues. The kids hung out in the motel room all day, pretty much exhausted. They just sat around watching TV, and then watching the adults get ready for the First Flight Ball.

"You look beautiful!" Christina exclaimed, when Mimi came out of the bathroom. She had on a black and white ball gown with her shiny blond hair all up on top of her head and sparkly earrings and necklace. With a wink, she lifted up her skirt and showed off her red satin dancing shoes.

Papa and Uncle Joe had on tuxedoes. "Penguin suits," Papa called them. He looked comfortable in his; Uncle Joe squirmed and tugged at his cummerbund, cuff links, and bow tie.

"Nothing like getting all gussied up only to go out in the rain," Mimi lamented. The rain and wind had slowed down to a drizzle. There was a knock on the door. "That's your sitter," Mimi said.

"What?!" cried Christina. "We're too old to have a baby sitter," she complained. The other kids nodded in agreement.

"I didn't say baby," Mimi said, "but after your recent venture, I'd feel better if you had company. It's Ned, the motel owner's son. He's 17. I think you can stand him for a few hours."

Christina knew there was no arguing, so she hugged her grandmother goodbye, wishing she were going to the ball, too.

The rest of the evening turned out not to be so bad after all. Ned brought a sack of microwave popcorn and some movies for the VCR. The kids decided he was pretty cool. He had lived on the Outer Banks all his life and knew a lot of neat trivia about Orville and Wilbur. He told them:
- Neither boy graduated from high school.
- They earned spending money by selling toys they made.
- Orville made a printing press out of parts of an old trombone and old buggies.

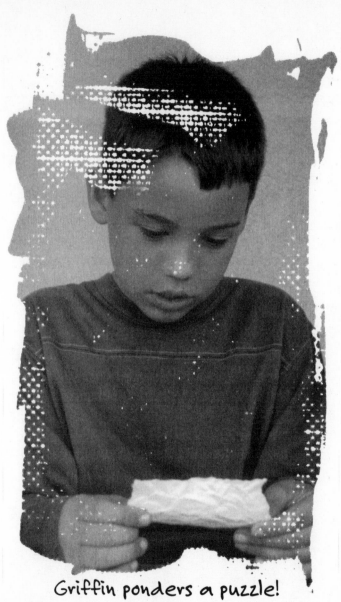

Griffin ponders a puzzle!

"What do you know about *Flyer*?" Christina asked.

Ned thought for a moment. "Well, I know it cost less than $1,000 to build. And I know it was made of wooden poles, baling wire, cloth, bike chains, and a gasoline engine that wasn't even as powerful as one on a lawn mower today!"

"Do you know where *Flyer* is?" Grant asked.

"Hey, you're not accusing me of anything, are you?" Ned asked, with a grin.

"Oh, no," Alex assured him. "We just want to find it."

"Doesn't everyone," Ned agreed. "It's supposed to be the highlight of the celebration tomorrow. Kitty Hawk will get bad publicity around the world if it isn't found."

Christina shook her head. It seemed impossible to find *Flyer* by tomorrow! But she wouldn't give up. She just wouldn't! And then, although he never knew it, Ned gave her the clue she so desperately needed.

"You know," Ned said. "I've been to a lot of Wright sites: Aviation Trail in Dayton, Ohio and the Wright Cycle Shop at the Henry Ford Museum in Dearborn, Michigan—why I think I could make a new *Flyer* if I had time before tomorrow," he bragged.

Christina gasped. She ran up to Ned and gave him a big hug. "Oh, Ned," she cried. "I'm not sure, but I think you may just have saved the First Flight Celebration!"

19

A RACE TO THE FINISH

Ned and the kids thought Christina was crazy. She would not tell them what her hunch about where *Flyer* was. Finally, they dozed off. When the adults tiptoed back in sometime after midnight, Papa slipped Ned a few dollars and the boy went back to the motel office.

The next thing Christina knew, it was already morning and the adults were up and dressed for the day's festivities.

"Where are Papa and Uncle Joe going?" Christina asked frantically, when she woke up and found the two men heading out the motel door with a wave goodbye.

"They're going to the memorial early," Mimi said. "Calm down! You kids have plenty of time to eat breakfast and get dressed. Then we'll go over before the traffic gets too bad."

Christina tugged open the drapes covering the window. She had thought it was still dark and rainy, but the sky was electric blue with no clouds in sight, and the sun was beaming down on the string of cars trickling bumper to bumper down the highway toward the Wright Brothers Memorial.

She heard a loud drone and saw a dark shadow pass overhead. It looked like a gigantic bat wing. "What's that?" she asked her grandmother.

Mimi glanced out the window. "Oh that's a spy plane. Cool, hey? It's just one of the airplanes in the flyover today. We won't want to miss that."

"But what about the first flight re-enactment?" Christina asked. Mimi just looked away and said nothing.

Christina woke up the other kids by bouncing on the bed. "Get up! Get up!" she called. "Today's the big day!"

Alex groaned and rolled over. "Are you going to tell us where you think *Flyer* is?" she asked Christina.

Mimi wheeled around. "What?!"

Christina gave in and told her grandmother what she thought. Mimi did not seem to believe her, not at all, whatsoever. "That's so farfetched!" she exclaimed, then added, "but at this point, we have nothing to lose but to go and see."

Soon, they were all dressed. They wore the new First Flight jackets and caps Papa and Uncle Joe had bought for them to wear today.

Mimi rushed them out the door and they hurried across the parking lot. "Oh, we'll never get there in time," she said, looking at the traffic moving at a snail's pace.

"I can take you!" Ned shouted. He had driven up behind them in his dune buggy. "Hey, you kids look cool!"

"We sure do!" agreed Grant, who was really proud of his new outfit. The rest of the kids just smiled and said, "Thanks."

Mimi looked at the contraption. "Well, I guess we could all crowd into that thing. It's not too far, and you can at least travel down the side of the road."

"We'll pass everything in sight!" Ned promised and the kids eagerly piled in the dune buggy. Mimi scooched in beside Ned and they zoomed off.

Christina was amazed at the sight before her. There were people everywhere. There were balloons and tents and souvenir stands and food concessions. Spread all across the grassy areas were airplanes of every age and era. Hot air balloons floated over the sound. Skydivers, trailing red, white, and blue smoke plumes, were landing one after the other on a big X near the museum. Everything and everyone was here, she thought, for the 100th anniversary of flight—everything except *Flyer*.

The kids just stood and gaped at the scene with their mouths hanging open. Not only had they never seen anything like this, but they thought they never would again. Soon, Mimi spied Papa and Uncle Joe. When she got their attention, she ran over to them and talked to them both at once. She waved her arms and pointed, as she told them about Christina's strange hunch that she knew where *Flyer* was. The men just frowned at her and shook their heads. But she got them each by an arm and tugged them over to where the children stood.

"Christina," Papa said. It was the voice he used when she was in trouble. "are you sure about this?"

Christina ducked her head and looked at the ground. Then she looked up and said, "I don't know Papa, but it could be. I promise it could. Can't we just go see?"

Papa and Uncle Joe looked at one another. They seemed agitated. Even aggravated. "Oh, ok," Papa said.

"But we have to hurry!" said Uncle Joe.

They climbed into Uncle Joe's Jeep and headed across a shortcut he knew to the little rundown village near the sound. People stared at them as they sped across the sand. Christina was so nervous she could hardly breathe.

When they got near the beat-up cottage where the three strange women lived, Uncle Joe stood up in the Jeep and stared straight ahead. Christina prayed she had not gotten everyone's hopes up only to be wrong. She would feel so stupid, if she was, she thought. But she would also be amazed if her hunch was correct.

"It is, I think it is. I think it really is!" Uncle Joe cried in excitement as they pulled up in front of the cottage. But it was not the cottage he was focused on —it was the windmill. Papa jumped out of the Jeep as soon as it stopped and the two men compared notes.

"Look!" said Papa. "That's gotta be the wings. And take a gander at the wood struts." Suddenly, he laughed. "Christina, come here!" he cried.

Christina ran to her grandfather. Was she right or was she wrong, she wondered. Papa gave her a big hug. "You did it, girl!" he cried. "Look—see what's driving the windmill? It's not wind at all! It's *Flyer's* motor!"

Suddenly, everyone was laughing and cheering. Mimi was crying. Uncle Joe was jumping up and down like a little kid. "So that's what they did with our tools," he said.

"How did you know the windmill was *Flyer*?" Alex asked Christina.

Christina grinned. "Grant's favorite TV show!" she said. "I always thought *Flyer* might be in plain sight . . . but I thought it would still be an airplane, not a windmill. But when I watched them making real stuff out of bits and pieces of junk, it stayed in my mind. And when Ned said he could make *Flyer* if he had time, then I just saw all the parts of the plane." Christina pointed at the windmill. "The cloth wings were just like the windmill's arms. And all those wooden pieces. I just wondered . . ."

But Christina never finished her sentence because the kids were jumping all over her, hugging her, and shaking her hand. "The plane was hidden in plain sight, wasn't it, Christina?" her brother marveled.

Watching the mechanics rebuild Flyer . . .

"I'm sure glad the hurricane didn't blow it down," Alex said.

Griffin said, "I'm sure glad we took that hang glider flight!"

Papa and Uncle Joe were banging at the cottage door. But then the three women ran out the back door and escaped in their rusty Jeep. "Should we chase them?" asked Mimi.

"No," said Uncle Joe. "Let's get *Flyer* back to the memorial. We just may be in time."

Papa found their tools on the back porch, and the men began to disassemble the windmill. Uncle Joe phoned for a park service truck, and soon they were piling the pieces in it. They hauled them back to the sandy spot where Uncle Joe's tent had once stood.

As the airshow got underway, Uncle Joe and Papa worked frantically. Soon, other mechanics showed up. Uncle Joe gave directions. Right before their eyes, a pile of sticks and cloth and a small motor turned into an airplane!

Uncle Joe glanced at his watch. "Get it into position, now!" he told the men.

"Don't you want to test it?" Papa asked.

"There's no time," said Uncle Joe. "We'll just have to do like Orville and Wilbur did—*try*!"

And then it was time. A narrow corridor across the dunes was cleared. The rest of the sandy hills was covered with spectators. The men participating in the re-enactment came forward. The narrator for the event spoke through a loud public address system. He had a very dramatic voice.

And now, ladies gentlemen. Go back! Go back in your mind 100 years ago. It was a cold winter's morning. It was the day that two brothers who had one dream—to fly!—had worked for all their lives.

Christina and the other kids held onto one another. Wind whipped their pants' legs. Mimi had tears streaming down her face. Papa stood behind them with his fingers crossed behind his back.

And here are the Wright brothers. They toss a coin.

As the narrator spoke, two men dressed in antique suits came forward and tossed a coin up into the air.

Orville will fly! The men shake hands. They crank the engine. Orville stretches out face-down on the bottom wing, which his brother holds steady. A helper releases the wire that holds Flyer to the ground.

The kids looked over in time to see Uncle Joe do this. Christina is certain that no one present is breathing. Except for the motor, it is silent on the dunes. Suddenly, *Flyer* begins to inch, then roll forward. It hesitates, then gains speed. Faster and faster. And then the plane is in the air. It is flying! It is flying! The kids look over at Uncle Joe and he gives them a big thumbs up! Almost instantly, the plane lands gently on the sand. There are thunderous cheers from the crowd!

That's history! That's just what happened 100 years ago, folks! The most famous 12 seconds in history. Just 120 feet (that's 37 meters)—but it was the First Flight!

20

FIRST FLIGHT

After the successful re-enactment, the spectators had cheered and cheered and cheered. Mimi and Papa and Uncle Joe had beamed like kids on Christmas morning. The kids were lost in the throng coming up to congratulate Uncle Joe and the men who had played the parts of Orville and Wilbur.

Soon, a large, dark car whisked up to them and a man in a black suit with a microphone in his ear opened the door. "Get in, please," he said. Christina could tell it was an order, not a request.

Because she was the closest, she got in first after Papa had nodded it was ok. The next thing Christina knew, she was sitting beside the First Lady. Across from her sat the President of the United States. "Congratulations, little lady," he said and reached out to shake Christina's hand.

The next morning, they were back at Manteo Airport. Papa and Uncle Joe were going over *My Girl's* pre-flight checklist. Christina was still in a daze. She, Mimi, and the other kids—even Ned, who had come to tell them goodbye—stood in the warm winter sun and waited.

"I still don't believe it," Christina said. "I shook hands with the president!"

"You shook—that's what you did!" Alex teased her. "Your hand was shaking like a leaf."

"Well, so was mine!" Mimi admitted.

They all had ridden in the presidential limousine back to a special tent (surrounded by Secret Service) for dignitaries and other special guests. Christina was astounded that they had been included. Uncle Joe had received a special recognition for his work on *Flyer*.

"What will happen to the mean women?" Grant asked Mimi.

"I'm not sure," said Mimi. "It's hard to believe that they were so angry about the first flight celebration that they wanted to steal *Flyer*. It seems they thought that their ancestors from that era had been shunned instead of being invited to participate."

Headed for home!

"Well, couldn't they just have complained?" Alex asked.

"I don't know," said Mimi. "I think they just made a string of bad decisions. But at least Papa's not going to jail!"

Papa looked over at Mimi and grinned. "No, Papa's not going to jail! He's going to Christmas—anyone coming with him?"

The kids all cheered and ran for the plane. Christina and Grant hugged Uncle Joe and Ned and Alex and Griffin goodbye and wished them a merry Christmas. Then, with Papa's help, they climbed into *My Girl* and fastened their seatbelts.

As the plane scooted down the runway, they waved to their friends on the ground. As those friends became tiny specks, Papa banked and the plane flew over the beautiful coastline. They were going home, and it was only a few days till Christmas. Christina settled back into her seat. "I know what I'm going to ask for for Christmas," she said.

"What?" asked Mimi and Papa together.

Christina laughed. "Flying lessons!"

"Me, too!" said Grant, turning his little arms into wings. "Me, toooooooooooo!"

Well, that was fun!

Wow, glad we solved that mystery!

Where shall we go next?

EVERYWHERE!

The End

Now...go to

www.carolemarshmysteries.com
and...

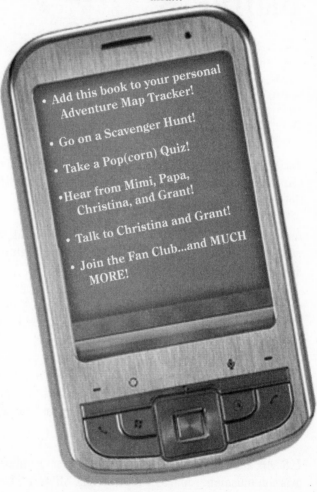

- Add this book to your personal Adventure Map Tracker!

- Go on a Scavenger Hunt!

- Take a Pop(corn) Quiz!

- Hear from Mimi, Papa, Christina, and Grant!

- Talk to Christina and Grant!

- Join the Fan Club...and MUCH MORE!

THE WRIGHT BROTHERS

Places To Go & Things To Know!

The Wright Brothers National Memorial, Kitty Hawk, North Carolina – Memorial, Museum, and Centennial of Flight Celebrations, culminating on December 17, 2003.

Aviation Trail, Dayton, Ohio – Self-guided tour highlighting various aviation landmarks in the Dayton area (features many of the sites listed here).

Carillon Historical Park, Dayton, Ohio – Original 1905 Wright Flyer 3, restored under Orville's supervision. Cycle shop replica, Barry Aviation Center & Wright Hall.

Dayton Aviation Heritage National Historical Park, Dayton, Ohio – Restored Wright Cycle Company building, Wright Brothers Print Shop building, Huffman Prairie Flying Field and Aviation Center.

U.S. Air Force Museum, Dayton, Ohio – Pioneer military aviation museum, replica of 1909 Wright Military Flyer, 1911

Wright Model B, National Aviation Hall of Fame.
Wright State University, Dayton Ohio – Special collections and archives are the most complete records of the lives and work of Orville and Wilbur Wright.

Engineer's Club of Dayton, Ohio – Orville was a founding member and past president of the club. The club has the 1904 Wright test engine and Orville's pilot's license (Number 1, issued by the USA Civil Aeronautics Authority).

Dayton-Wright Brothers Airport, Miamisburg, Ohio – Home of the Wright Flyer B Hangar. Houses 2 flying replicas of 1910-1914 Wright Model Bs, the first production airplane. With reservations, visitors can actually fly in one!

Henry Ford Museum and Greenfield Village,
Dearborn, Michigan – The original Wright Cycle Shop and their boyhood home, moved from Dayton.

The Franklin Institute, Philadelphia, Pennsylvania – The largest collection of artifacts from the Wright brothers' workshops, donated by Orville. Airfoils, windtunnels, engines and aircraft drawings.

The National Air and Space Museum, Washington, D.C. – (Part of the Smithsonian) See the original 1903 *Flyer*!

www.first-to-fly.com – The virtual Wright Brothers Aeroplane Company and Museum of Pioneer Aviation. Very extensive online museum, historical guide, and archives for kids about everything Wright!

GLOSSARY

causeway: a roadway over water between two pieces of land

counterpane: and old-fashioned type of patchwork quilt

Eureka: meaning "I found it" or figured it out

gallivant: to go from place to place

palisade: a fort made with walls, usually of wooden posts

port: meaning the left side or "to the left"

pummel: to beat up on

starboard: meaning the right side or "to the right"

Tarheel: nickname for a person from North Carolina

tarmac: the paved areas of an airport

SAT GLOSSARY

descendants: someone's children, grandchildren, great-grandchildren, etc.

involuntary: not done consciously or on purpose

maritime: related to the sea

replica: something built to look just like the original

simultaneous: at the same time

Enjoy this exciting excerpt from:

THE MYSTERY ON THE Freedom Trail

1

WHAT IN THE WORLD IS A BM ANYWAY?

"Boston is a long way from Georgia," Christina mused as she read the curious white note with the red lining once again. "I guess we'd have to take an airplane."

Christina Yother, 9, a fourth-grader in Peachtree City, Georgia, her brother, Grant, 7, and their Grandmother Mimi stood around the bright red mailbox. They ignored the bills, advertisements, and the little box of free detergent stuffed in the mailbox to concentrate on the invitation to visit Boston. The invitation read:

> Mimi,
>
> You and your two delightful grandchildren are invited to visit us during the big BM! Cousins Derian and C.F. will enjoy showing the kids Bean Town! Let me know ASAP. Patriots' Day is coming soon, you know!
>
> Love,
> Emma

Mimi tapped the note with her bright red fingernail. "I guess Patriots' Day *is* coming soon. Today is the last day of March.   She could have given us a little more notice."

Of course, Christina knew that didn't really matter to her Grandmother Mimi.   She was not like most grandmothers. She wasn't really like a grandmother at all. She had bright blond hair, wore all the latest sparkly clothes, was the CEO of her own company, and took off for parts unknown at a moment's notice.

"Aunt Emma sure likes exclamation points," observed Christina. "Just like you, Mimi!"

"You bet!" said Mimi, giving her granddaughter's silky, chestnut-colored hair a tousle.   "I'm the Exclamation Mark Queen!" She looked down at Grant who was fingering the corner of the invitation. He looked very serious.   "What's wrong, Grant?" asked Mimi.

Even standing on the curb, Grant was small. His blue eyes seemed the biggest part of him. He looked up at his grandmother. "Well, for one thing, Aunt Emma sure uses a lot of letters instead of words. What does ASAP stand for?"

Christina knew that one. (Of course, she always did!) "It means As Soon As Possible—right, Mimi?"

"That's right," said Mimi. "You can say A-S-A-P, or say it like a word—asap."

"Then I hate to be a sap and ask the next question," said Grant with a sigh.

"What's that?" asked Mimi. "There are no dumb questions, you know."

Grant slid off the curb, looking littler than ever. "It's not the question that bothers me . . . it's the possible answer. I mean what *is* a big BM?"

Mimi laughed. "Not what you apparently think it means! The BM is the Boston Marathon. It's the biggest deal in Boston each year. People come from all over the world to run in this race."

"Oh," Grant said with a grin. He looked relieved, and so did his sister. "So it's like the Peachtree Road Race on the 4th of July?"

"Sort of," said Mimi, folding the note and stuffing it back in its envelope. "Only the Boston Marathon is the oldest marathon in America, so it's really special. It has an incredible history!"

Christina and Grant grabbed one another and groaned. Oh, no! When Mimi said the word *history*, they knew they would be in for a big, long tale of everything about everything. But not this time. She ignored her grandkids' dramatic groaning and headed up the driveway for the house.

Christina chased her, running beneath the overhang of magnolia limbs over the azalea-lined path of pink and purple blooms. "Are we going?"

Grant chased Christina. "Wait up, you two!" he pleaded. He took a shortcut across the wide green lawn, weaving (against Mimi's rules) through the forest of pampas grass spewing fountains of white, feathery spikes. "Are we going?" he begged.

On the front porch, Mimi plopped down in the big, white Victorian rocking chair. She pulled out her cell phone from her jacket pocket. Grant and Christina piled into the rocker beside her. "Are we? Are we?!" they hissed, as Mimi dialed the number. They held their breath until they heard her say, "Emma? We're coming to the Big BM!"

After Mimi hung up the phone, she jiggled the other rocking chair, causing the two kids to giggle. "What's wrong, Grant?" she asked. "You still don't look happy!"

Grant looked at his grandmother thoughtfully. "If we go to Boston, do we get to eat anything beside beans?"